THE ART OF THE DEAL

B. A. STRETKE

Dreamspinner Press

Published by
Dreamspinner Press
5032 Capital Circle SW
Ste 2, PMB# 279
Tallahassee, FL 32305-7886
USA
http://www.dreamspinnerpress.com/

The Art of the Deal

Cover Art by Aaron Anderson
aaronbydesign55@gmail.com

ISBN: 978-1-62380-424-4
Digital ISBN: 978-1-62380-425-1

Printed in the United States of America
First Edition
April 2013

In memory of my aunt Joanne K. Burtt. She never lost faith in me and was always there to fight in my corner.

Aunt Jo, you are dearly loved and will be missed more than you'll ever know. Requiescat in Pace.

ONE

SEAN ROBBINS stood with the other four students in front of the selection committee at the university luncheon, feeling anxious and hopeful. The luncheon had been arranged to honor the top five students from the legal studies program. Because of their academic achievement, they had been selected for prestigious summer placements at Coleman West and Associates law firm in Chicago. The positions lasted through the summer session and counted as a complete semester's course work. A successful placement at the Coleman West firm virtually guaranteed the students a job anywhere they chose after graduation. An internship certificate signed by Coleman West was considered golden.

Coleman West, the owner of the firm, was a valued member of the board of regency of the university. For the past four years, those five educational placements had been made available to the top achievers in legal studies. Professor Timothy Weir had told this year's group that every student who had attained one of the placements and completed it successfully had gone on to good, high-paying careers. The top student earned the coveted placement with Coleman himself. That placement was the toughest yet the most sought after. A placement with Coleman usually resulted in employment with the firm following the completion of the internship.

Sean was both proud and excited about the future he envisioned. As the top student, Sean was to receive the placement with Coleman. Weir had assured him his placement with Coleman was secure. Sean couldn't wait to meet him and learn all the details. It was such a remarkable opportunity to meet one of the best in the legal profession and learn from them. Coleman had an impeccable reputation. His firm had represented large businesses, politicians, and celebrities, yet he also donated time to low income clients through his pro-bono work. Sean had never met him but he had read plenty and was thoroughly impressed with the man and his work. Working with him and learning from him would probably prove to be the high point of his life.

All of these thoughts ran anxiously through his mind as he stood waiting for Weir to distribute the placements. He wanted to get the show on the road. They were to begin their placements on Monday. Sean was already packed and ready to leave. The firm was approximately four hours away, so Sean and his classmates would have to relocate for the duration of the internship. The firm provided housing for the interns, so rent wouldn't be an issue and paid them the standard beginning legal-assistant wage as a stipend. He had nothing to worry about financially, and he was looking forward to a fun and rewarding experience.

He was pulled abruptly from his thoughts when his classmate Brittany Saunders was called forward and the professor handed her a scroll. Only Coleman's intern received a scroll; everyone else got a certificate. The professor had given her the position of legal intern to Coleman. Before Sean had a chance to process what he'd heard, Weir called his name and gave him the position of legal intern to Edward Murray. The name wasn't familiar to Sean, who had researched the entire Coleman West firm; Murray wasn't one of the associates. *Who in the hell is Edward Murray*, he wanted to yell. He wanted to demand an explanation, but he said nothing. He schooled his features to show no reaction and hid how upset he was. He kept his eyes trained on a little old lady sitting at the head table; she smiled at him and that helped. His control slipped back into place.

Brittany gave Sean a hateful grin and whispered, "Not as smart as you thought you were," as she brought the scroll to her lips and pretended to kiss it.

Sean and Brittany had been adversaries since the beginning of the program. Brittany had always been given the best of everything. Opportunities were her right, and they had always come to her effortlessly until Sean came along and moved in on her territory. She was the class star and the teachers' favorite until Sean showed up. The fact that Sean had beaten her for the top placement had caused Brittany to throw a tantrum—the likes of which her family and friends had never witnessed before. Now, according to Brittany, everything was back to normal: Sean has been put in his place publicly, and Brittany was again on top.

Sean said nothing. He was confused and embarrassed. He had worked hard to maintain his grades in order to get the top position. This couldn't be happening. Weir was a fair man; there had to be a reason. Everyone knew Sean was to have the position with Coleman, and now he had to stand here in front of everyone as the position was given to someone else. This was one of the most humiliating moments of his life. The expressions of the audience in the room were judging and speculating; it was too hard to look, so Sean once again stared at the old woman at the head table. She gave him a warm, comforting smile, which he once again appreciated. Weir leaned over and whispered to Sean to meet him in his office after the luncheon.

The professor had told him just yesterday that he had placed him with Coleman. Why would he change his mind? Sean knew his grade point average was higher than Brittany's. She knew it too. She had demanded a recount and the numbers were checked twice. He exceeded her numbers by .028; it wasn't a lot, but it put him in front. So why had Brittany gotten the top spot? Even more perplexing than that was the mysterious Murray. Sean would have to wait. He tried to stand as tall as his slight five-foot-eight-inch frame would al ow. Gathering all the strength he had, he held his head up and locked everyone in the eyes. He knew that was important. *Don't let them shake you; don't let them see your vulnerabilities.* He'd learned that lesson at a very early age.

Once the luncheon had finally ended, Sean moved toward Weir, who motioned for him to follow him. He pushed his wavy brown hair back behind one ear and pinned him with his dark-green eyes. The professor looked sad and disappointed. Sean didn't know what to expect when he sat down across from him in his office. The professor sat behind his desk and regarded Sean silently for a few moments.

"I'm sorry, Sean," he began and dropped his gaze to his desktop. "Coleman West rejected your application."

Sean was speechless for a moment, then said, "Why? Did he say why?"

"No, he didn't, he just wrote that you were unsuitable."

Sean knew there had to be more to it, but he assumed that Weir was too nice to tell him.

"Who is Edward Murray, and why is he willing to have me if Mr. West considers me unsuitable?" His voice was tight and strained; he was so hurt by the obviously *personal* nature of this rejection.

"Ed is an acquaintance of mine, and I asked him to take you on as an assistant," the professor explained in the same tense whisper Sean was using. "Ed isn't a partner—he's part of the pool—but he is a fine lawyer. You will get a good experience with him."

"Why would he accept me after West said no? Won't he get into trouble with the boss?" Sean's tone became crisp and clipped as anger replaced hurt.

"One of the reasons Ed has never made partner is because he follows his own path. He does what's right, not what's politically correct, and that's also why he accepted you. He looked at your performance record and agreed you had earned a placement at the firm.'

"What if Coleman West finds out I'm there?" Sean asked, still disheartened. "He can still have me removed, and he probably will."

"That's a risk I believe you'll be willing to take."

Just then the professor was called from the room by a needy, impatient student in the hallway. It gave Sean an opportunity to get a closer look at the white envelope tucked partially under the professor's desk calendar. Sean was very adept at reading upside down and backward, and he easily recognized the Coleman West law firm logo. He didn't have time to read the contents, so he quickly hid the letter in his backpack and returned the empty envelope to its place before Weir returned to the room.

Sean felt tense and confused. He thought the internship had been a given; the highest grade got the prime placement. Every intern placed with Coleman West as his personal intern went on to work for his firm. He had allowed himself to believe that would be his future. He hadn't considered that his application might be rejected. What had been wrong with his application? He had gone over every word again and again. What had he written that Coleman took exception to?

"I'm okay. I'll do fine with Mr. Murray. Don't worry," Sean said to reassure the professor when he returned.

"I'm sorry, Sean." Weir said. "I'm so sorry… I wish—" He didn't have a chance to finish before Sean shot to his feet and left the office. He ran from the building and went to his favorite spot. It was on a small hill on the edge of campus, and from there he had a view of Mt. Pleasant. Sean pulled the letter from his backpack and slowly unfolded the expensive stationary.

Dear Professor Weir,

I recently received your recommendations for internship placements at this firm. As always, your students appear to be top rate. I will gladly accept four of the five candidates. Unfortunately I cannot accept Mr. Sean Robbins. Based on the content of his application, I find there to be a distinct lack of proper character. He is completely unsuitable for a position at this firm. I'm sure that with his grades and abilities he will go far within his limited social structure, but there is no place for him here at the firm.

Sincerely,

Coleman West

Sean read the letter over and over, stunned by the arrogance and prejudice it contained. Coleman was nothing, *nothing* like what Sean had thought. He was narrow and limited and... mean. "This is unbelievable," Sean mumbled. The man was pure garbage. Sean chastised himself for ever thinking Coleman was someone special. At that moment, there wasn't anyone in the world that he despised more than Coleman. He refolded the letter and put it back into his pack.

Sean's plan was to complete the ten-week placement with Murray and then get the hell out of there. He didn't need Coleman; he didn't need anyone. He would make it with sheer dogged determination, if not with his own personal skill.

ED MURRAY'S office was on the third floor of the eight-floor office building. Sean found it was easy to avoid the associates and the other students he had been in class with. Coleman and all his partners had their offices on the eighth floor. Quite the pretentious bunch, he'd discovered. Ed was a really good guy. He worked with low-income clients and pro-bono cases more than any other lawyer at the firm. He treated everyone the same, with the same level of respect and consideration. Sean was glad he had been placed with Ed. He was getting valuable experience, and Ed was letting him actually work the cases with him like a real assistant.

Ed was a man in his forties who had spent his entire legal career helping others and in the process had made very little money. He had come to the Coleman West and Associates law firm five years earlier. He'd started on the third floor, and he was still on the third floor. He was married to his high school sweetheart and had three children, all of whom were currently in law school. Ed was a stark contrast to Coleman. Sean decided he was fortunate to be working with someone with the moral caliber of Ed. Coleman could never understand a kind, ethical, decent man like Ed. Sean acknowledged that he was glad on some level that Coleman had rejected him. He didn't care that he'd had to find a one-room apartment so far from downtown it took him over half an hour on a bus to get to work every morning. And he didn't care that, unlike the other interns, he was paid only minimum wage. He appreciated the fact that Ed was able to pay him anything at all, considering it came out of his own pocket. Coleman gave him nothing because Sean was not a Coleman intern; he was an Ed's intern and proud of it.

The first time Sean caught a glimpse of Coleman was a few days after he started. He was in the parking garage in the basement of the building, getting some paperwork from Ed's car, when Coleman pulled in. Sean recognized him from a vain portrait of himself with the four other partners hanging in the lobby entrance. Coleman drove an impressive black Mercedes. A man with that magnitude of self-love wouldn't be satisfied with anything less, Sean thought snidely. It was all looks for his kind. Sean had ducked down beside Ed's car as Coleman drove by and parked in his private space next to the elevators. Sean watched him from his hiding place.

"Pompous jerk," he mumbled, although he was impressed with what he saw despite himself. Coleman was very tall, well over six feet, and lean and muscular. His hair was shiny, black, and combed back from his face. His face was firm and rather angular, with a pronounced brow line, which made him appear very intense, and he had high cheekbones, a square jaw, and piercing, coal-black eyes. He paused and surveyed the area as if he knew someone was watching him. Sean ducked down further and waited to hear the elevator before risking another peek. When he ventured another glance, Coleman was walking into the elevator. He was dressed in an immaculately cut black suit, probably very expensive. Sean admitted to himself that if he hadn't despised him so much, he would have found him quite handsome.

SEAN had been on the job a full month before he had the misfortune of coming face-to-face with Coleman. He was a confirmed bachelor, according to the receptionist in the lobby. She told Sean that Coleman was usually seen with a different person every week. He definitely played the field, but only went out with the cream of society. So Sean assumed that the title "confirmed bachelor" was simply code for "manwhore." As far as Sean knew, Coleman valued nothing but himself and his money. He was fast and cold in his judgments and assessments, and no one was ever given a second chance. Everyone who worked for him knew that to cross him meant you would instantly be looking for employment elsewhere. He did not tolerate insubordination from anyone for any reason, and there were no exceptions in his world. Sean was very surprised, and at first didn't believe it, when he was told Coleman was of the same sexual orientation as himself. Sean was certain part of the reason he had been rejected was because Coleman had somehow found out he was gay. But why would that be an issue if Coleman himself were gay?

Ed had assured him he would probably never run into Coleman because he never concerned himself with third-floor business. "He's a top-floor man, Sean. You'll never lay eyes on him." Sean remembered those words clearly as he stood staring into the eyes of the man he had been told he would probably never see. It was just before eight o'clock in the morning, and he was racing across the lobby to catch the elevator that would take him to the third floor. He liked to arrive a little early in order to have Ed's office open and coffee brewing by the time he arrived.

Coleman had seen him rushing to the elevator and was very graciously holding the door for him. Sean never would've expected such consideration from the likes of Coleman. Sean had never seen him on these elevators before. Coleman usually used the private elevator behind the reception area. Sean froze at the elevator's entrance and just stared at him. He couldn't breathe and a sense of panic washed over him. He felt as if he'd been punched in the gut. When Coleman smiled at him it seemed to break the spell, and Sean backed up quickly, shaking his head as he spoke.

"No... thank you," he mumbled awkwardly, and without another word, he turned abruptly on his heels and ran for the stairwell.

Coleman watched him as he ran away from him. He was both puzzled and intrigued by the young man's behavior.

Sean was panicking and out of breath by the time he reached Ed's office. He dropped his bag on the desk and sat down heavily. His thoughts careened in many directions at once. "Shit, shit, shit!" he burst through clenched teeth. *Did he recognize me? Does he know what I look like? Does he know I'm here at the firm? Is he going to have me removed? Shit, shit, shit.*

Thankfully, he managed to compose himself by the time Ed arrived for work. Sean decided not to mention the incident to him; Ed had enough on his mind already. No one had come to remove him yet, so perhaps it was just good manners that had made Coleman hold the door for him. Coleman hadn't recognized him; if he had, he wouldn't have waited this long to deal with him. He would have had security remove him by now. Sean relaxed a little and decided he needed to be a little more diligent about keeping out of the boss man's way. "I have to be more careful," he told himself out loud. *Stay on the edges; stay in the shadows.* Sean was afraid that not only would he seal his own fate if caught, but he could also ruin Ed's career here at Coleman West and Associates.

Sean had trouble getting Coleman out of his mind. He hadn't expected him to be considerate. Coleman had smiled at Sean, but then, he was a manwhore; he probably smiled at every person he thought might be available. Even though Sean knew that probably wasn't true, he needed to put Coleman back in a bad light in his thoughts and not think of him as the nice guy who'd kindly held the elevator doors for him. Though Coleman appeared pleasant enough, Sean knew better and had to keep in mind that the man would toss Sean's ass out in a heartbeat if he caught him here. Coleman did not tolerate the presence of low-class scum on his premises. "Stay focused, Sean," he reminded himself.

COLEMAN was having an equally difficult time getting that young man out of his thoughts. No one had ever looked at him with such revulsion and dread. Coleman had seen the young man several times over the past couple of weeks, and he always seemed to go out of his way to avoid him, like he had today. The younger man would rather take the stairs than share an elevator with him. The more he ran away from him, the more intrigued Coleman became. Coleman had spent days trying to meet and speak with him, but he was too quick. This morning the timing was perfect. Coleman knew he worked in the building and assumed he arrived at eight o'clock, so he waited by the elevators for him to come across the lobby. This was Coleman's chance to have the young man in a confined space for a few minutes and introduce himself. But that hadn't worked out. Coleman's presence had stopped him in his tracks, and he'd just stared at him and then run for the stairwell.

"What did I ever do to him to elicit such a reaction?" he said to himself as he looked out the large window in his office. From his vantage point on the top floor, Coleman could see the entire waterfront. The morning sun shone on the water, glistening and bouncing on the gentle waves. He continued to think about that man. Coleman couldn't get him out of his mind. Did he work for him in some capacity? Had he heard some of the terrible stories about him that circulated continually and got larger and more heinous with each telling? And was that why he seemed to be scared to death of him? The young man seemed sickened by the prospect of spending even a few minutes alone in an elevator with him. His thoughts returned to the same question: What could he have done that had left such an impression on this man, while he, Coleman, didn't recognize him?

Coleman was abruptly pulled out of his thoughts by the voice of his secretary on the intercom announcing his first appointment of the day.

"Good morning," Jason said as he closed the door behind him and took a seat on the small leather sofa. Coleman poured him a cup of coffee and handed it to him. Jason Weintaub was one of the senior partners and had been with Coleman West and Associates since Coleman first took over the firm from his father six years earlier. They had been good friends since law school.

"It is a beautiful day," Coleman commented as he sat down across from Jason in a leather chair. "I think I might take a walk during lunch," he offered idly.

"Wow, you're in a good mood." Jason smiled broadly. Jason was single and near Coleman's age of thirty-two years. They often spent their leisure time together and had even double-dated on occasion.

Coleman rarely dated anyone more than once or twice. He feared commitment and refused to be tied to anyone. His parents' marriage had been a disaster from the start. They had been divorced since Coleman was four years old. His father had retired and was currently married to his fifth wife; his mother had divorced her third husband three months ago and at present was engaged to her divorce lawyer. Throughout his life Coleman had learned to accept and discard an ever-changing parade of stepmothers and fathers. He saw no permanence in relationships, and he was adamant that he would never marry, never commit himself to anyone. He had once stated, very coldly, that people were much easier to discard if there was no paperwork involved. A lesson learned from his parents, no doubt.

"What's given you such a sunny point of view this morning?" Jason laughed. "Is there a new man in your life?" he teased and was shocked by Coleman's response.

"Yes, there is," he stated emphatically.

"Who is he?" Jason had been joking when he asked his original question. Coleman didn't get dreamy or excited over any man, ever. Easy come and easy go was how he saw all of his personal relationships. Having him state that there was a special man who was affecting his mood in a positive manner was tantamount to him saying that pigs flew and little green men from Mars had just invaded the office. Coleman respected people in the workplace, but as far as companionship went, he preferred his own. Personal, romantic relationships were strictly for entertainment purposes; Jason sat and waited for him to elaborate on the individual responsible for the smile he was witnessing.

"I don't know his name, but I think he works here in some capacity." Coleman leaned forward, resting his forearms on his thighs as if he were going to relay important, private information. "I saw him in the parking garage and then in the lobby over the course of a couple of mornings. Each time I try to approach him he runs away, or so it seems." He laughed. He didn't tell Jason about the elevator incident; he wasn't sure why.

"What does he look like? Maybe I know his name," Jason offered. He watched as Coleman thought and he saw a pleased expression come to his face as he began to describe the man.

"The guy has wavy brown hair that hangs just below his ears but is impeccably styled. He has the most beautiful, striking green eyes I have ever seen. He's about five foot seven or eight, but what he lacks in height he makes up for in attitude. He carries himself like a professional, like a man secure in who he is. The guy is probably early to midtwenties, I'd guess." Coleman laughed out loud. "It's crazy, I don't know anything about this man, not even his name, and yet he is the most compelling individual I've come across in a long time."

"You are really surprising me." Jason sat back and stared at his friend. "Why do you find this guy so interesting?"

"I don't know; there's just something about him."

"Well, he sounds a little like the intern working with Murray."

Coleman drew his eyebrows together. "Ed has an intern?" Jason nodded. "From what school?"

Jason shrugged in the universal sign of "I don't know."

"There are only two schools that have interns here, and they are all placed with upper-level people." He thought for a moment and then stated his thoughts. "Three from Cooley University and four of the five from St. Mary's University."

"Why only four of the five? I thought you always accepted the interns from SMU," Jason asked idly.

"Weir usually has the best students, and he has always sent me stellar candidates for internships, but this time," he said as he sat back in the chair and rolled his eyes, "he sent me an application from a young man who would have been more appropriately placed in the local bar."

Now this is the Coleman he was used to—hard and judgmental with a hint of cruelty. "What was wrong with him?"

"First off, he was a returning student. Apparently, he couldn't cut it the first time around. Came back to school after a year of doing God knows what and began a two-year legal studies degree."

"Weren't his grades up to par? Weir usually has a stipulation on grade point to get an internship here," Jason interjected.

"Oh, his grades were the highest in the class, but that fact does not negate the previous drop-out status, or the fact that he was putting himself through school by working at the local nightclub." Coleman was incensed that someone like that had even attempted to receive a placement with his firm. "I have a reputation to maintain, and there is no room for a common bar slut in my organization." He remembered the letter of rejection he'd sent back to Professor Weir, which in no uncertain terms made it clear that he had best never again try to send him a student such as Sean Robbins. He had committed the name to memory in case the young man ever tried to get employment with his firm or any of his affiliates or friends. Coleman West had destroyed the career aspirations of people before whom he deemed as unacceptable, and he planned on doing the same for Mr. Sean Robbins.

Jason and Coleman then turned their attention to their pending cases and spent the next two hours working through the fine points of a malpractice suit that Jason was scheduled to argue that afternoon. During lunch, Coleman made good on his desire to take a walk and walked down to the third floor. He wanted to get a look at Ed's intern and see if he was his mystery man. Unfortunately, they were both in court when he arrived. No one seemed to know his name, yet they had nothing but positive things to say about him. He sounded like a very capable assistant, so Coleman wondered why he hadn't been placed elsewhere in the firm. How had Ed gotten an intern?

Ed had worked for him for the past five years. He was an excellent lawyer, but had no desire to rise in the ranks, no desire to make it big, and he loved hardship cases. Coleman wasn't sure he understood the man, but he respected him.

Coleman described the young man to several people on the third floor, and they all agreed that it sounded like Ed's intern. He returned to his office after he was informed that Ed and his assistant would be out of the office until after three.

TWO

"JOANNA," Coleman said to his personal secretary, "arrange a luncheon for the interns and their supervisors for Friday." As he walked into his office, he stopped and spoke to her again. "Have internship lapel pins and certificates made." Later, he buzzed her on the intercom and added, "Notify all the supervisors by e-mail except Ed Murray. I'll tell him in person."

SEAN was glad to be out of the building with Ed for a few hours. He now constantly feared running into Coleman again. If he ran away again, Coleman would definitely take offense but what would he say if Coleman asked him questions? *He won't talk to me.* He chastised himself for believing Coleman would be interested in him enough to ask his name. *He doesn't care about the average worker at the firm.* Sean relaxed a little when he realized how absurd he was being thinking that Coleman would actually talk to him. *Just stay out of his view and stay away from the elevators.*

COLEMAN decided to surprise Ed and just show up at his office unannounced. Part of him was concerned that if he called first the intern would find some way to disappear before he arrived. He still could not, for the life of him, understand why the young man kept avoiding him. He would surprise him and whatever the problem, he would try to make amends. It couldn't have been anything too serious. Coleman was adamant in his desire to know this man's name.

SEAN was in the back office, preparing paperwork for a case Ed would be presenting on Friday. He had finally managed to put the disturbing thoughts of Coleman out of his mind and was quite enjoying the research assigned to him. Sean liked it here with Ed, who was a very good teacher with plenty to share and a knack for skillfully getting information across to him. As he was reading, he suddenly became aware of voices in the outer office. Sean recognized Ed's but was unfamiliar with the other voice. Ed was answering questions and explaining himself in such a way that led Sean to believe the other person was his superior. Sean tensed and hoped it was one of the senior partners down here, checking on a specific case or something. He kept his fingers crossed. All hope drained away, though, when Ed came to the doorway of the back office with a pained look on his face.

"Mr. West would like to meet my intern." There was a small window in the south wall of the small office, and as Sean glanced toward it, Ed smiled and said, "You'd get stuck, son. Come on I'll go with you." He indicated for Sean to follow him.

Sean followed as Ed led him out to the main office area, where Coleman stood, tall and dark and as impressive as ever. Their gazes locked, and a smile instantly came to Coleman's lips, which took Sean by surprise. Coleman stepped forward with his hand outstretched. Sean looked at him and his hand and felt the blood drain from his face. Slowly, he put his hand out, and Coleman instantly grabbed it in a firm yet friendly grip.

"Hello, I'm Coleman West. I don't believe we've met, formally." He added the last because they had indeed met before. His voice was very deep and commanding. Sean held Coleman's hand and felt the firm grip and the warmth of his grasp. He could now see the man had deep green eyes, in which Sean lost himself. Coleman smiled, reveling in the contact, and waited for him to introduce himself.

It took a few moments for Sean to respond. Many things were running through his mind. He considered a false name, but he wasn't a very good liar. He thought perhaps he should lead with an apology, but that wasn't him either. Why apologize? He wasn't sorry he'd done this; he was sorry he gotten caught.

Coleman held his hand and waited. He saw several emotions playing across the man's face. He looked anxious, fearful like a trapped animal almost. But there was a strength-filled pride that was also present in the way he stood and the way he held his head and never looked away from him.

"No sir, we've not met formally," he began very softly, and Coleman took another step toward him, still holding his grasp and his gaze. "My name is Sean Robbins."

Sean watched closely as the smile fell from Coleman's face, but he didn't look angry. He looked shocked by Sean's declaration. His grip tightened, and he took another step toward Sean, so they were mere inches apart. Sean wanted to back away, to put more distance between them, but he also knew he had to hold his ground. He couldn't be perceived as weak, not now. Coleman covered Sean's hand with his own. The gesture was friendly and comforting, and truly unexpected. He looked at Sean's face for a long moment, as though searching for something, and then he smiled, though it seemed laced with sadness.

"I'm pleased to meet you, Sean," Coleman said very clearly, and he let his hand travel up Sean's arm to rest on his shoulder, which he squeezed before repeating, "I'm very pleased to meet you." Coleman continued to stare, not really sure he'd heard the man correctly, almost waiting for him to laugh and tell him his real name. But no, the man stood and waited; he seemed to be bracing himself for the worst. The grasp of his hand remained firm and sure.

Sean waited for the attack, the cut down, but Coleman just held his hand and continued to study him. Sean gradually managed to disengage from his grip and stepped back, putting a few feet between them. He had turned to go to the back office when Coleman spoke to him again.

"Sean," Coleman said with firm determination in his voice. Sean stopped and waited, but didn't turn to face him. "I'm glad you're here," Coleman finally said. Sean didn't respond but remained motionless for a few moments and then quickly escaped into the back office and closed the door behind him. Sean leaned against the door, shaking from the encounter. Coleman was an imposing and powerful presence. Now he understood why people feared him. As he looked around the small office, Sean accepted the fact that he would not be returning to it tomorrow. Coleman would have it out with Ed first and hopefully not fire him, but it was a surety that he would have Sean dismissed before the day was over.

AS SOON as Sean left the room, Coleman turned his attention to Ed. He didn't speak; he riveted him with a stare and waited for Ed to explain.

"I know Tim Weir," Ed began. "He asked me to supervise Sean. He said Sean is the best he's seen in years, and he needed to be given a fair chance. I checked Sean's performance record, and I agreed. I don't know why you rejected him, that isn't my business, but he deserves a placement even if it is just with me here on the third floor. I take full responsibility for my conduct in this matter."

Ed stood and waited to be told the consequences of his actions. Coleman didn't abide people who went against his judgments and his orders. Ed had taken on Sean because it was the right thing to do, and he had no regrets regarding that decision, even if it meant losing his position at the firm.

Coleman listened to Ed with irritation at first, his old feelings concerning possible insubordination coming to the forefront. Ed had gone expressly against his wishes by accepting this particular student, but he'd done it for the best reasons, and Coleman could respect that.

"You're a good man, Ed," Coleman said with respect and a profound admiration for the man. He put out his hand and shook Ed's. Coleman was impressed with Ed's sense of duty to his fellow man. He had known that by taking on Sean, he was risking his own job, and yet he did the right thing anyway. He would always do the right thing.

Colman decided to let the entire matter drop and not make an issue of the placement. Besides, his only concern at the moment was getting to know Sean better. He explained to Ed about the scheduled luncheon on Friday and asked for both of them to attend.

Sean came out of the back room as soon as he was sure Coleman had left. "Did he tell you to get rid of me?" he asked, disheartened.

"Quite the contrary," Ed declared. "We've been invited to a luncheon on Friday for the interns and their supervisors."

"What? A lunch?" Sean was incredulous. "Did he yell at you for accepting me as your intern after he had rejected my application? He couldn't have been very pleased." Sean was searching for explanations, but Ed wasn't very forthcoming.

"He didn't yell, and he seems perfectly fine with you being here."

"Wow, what does that mean? It's pretty strange considering the stories I've heard about the man. I was expecting a rather ugly scene, actually." Sean pondered his situation for another moment before seeking further clarification. "So I am allowed to continue here… as your intern?"

"Yeah, he didn't say anything about either of us leaving." Ed smiled broadly and patted Sean on the shoulder. "It will all be fine, son, don't worry."

COLEMAN walked back to his office, so caught up in his own thoughts he completely ignored two people who were trying to speak to him. He simply entered his office in silence and closed his door behind him. "He's beautiful," he said out loud to himself as he once again gazed out his window at Lake Michigan. Sean was the most handsome and compelling individual he'd met in years. Coleman glanced down at his right hand, remembering his touch. Holding Sean's hand had actually felt energizing, so much so he had resisted releasing him. Coleman smiled to himself. Sean was so strong willed, so secure in himself, and had seemed well aware that Coleman could have had him thrown out. Coleman had done worse things to people who had done less, but Sean hadn't flinched. He had seemed prepared to take whatever Coleman dished out. Once he knew he was caught, he'd faced him, unwaveringly so. "Yes, the most impressive man I've met in quite some time," Coleman stated out loud.

He turned away from the window and sat down at his desk, feeling suddenly small and petty. Coleman reached into one of the bottom drawers and pulled out all of the intern applications. He thumbed through them until he found the one for Sean. Coleman laid it on the desktop and returned the others to the bottom drawer. What was it about Sean's application that had led him to treat him so harshly? Sean was a returning student, and he worked part time at a local nightclub. Coleman took the time to read the application closer. He read the attached narrative, which explained the reason for the break in his education. Sean stated in his narrative only that he left school for a family obligation. He had not elaborated any further. Coleman was suddenly consumed with the need to learn all he could about Sean. Coleman dug through his papers and found the good professor's phone number.

"Hello, Professor Weir please," he said formally to the woman who answered the professor's phone.

"May I say who is calling?" she asked politely.

"Coleman West," he stated sharply. Coleman was promptly placed on hold.

"Hello, Mr. West. How can I help you?" Professor Weir said almost immediately.

Coleman explained the situation with Sean and asked for clarification with regard to his application.

"He deserved the placement—" Weir pressed in to drive his opinion home, but Coleman cut him off before he could continue.

"I agree," he stated impatiently. "What I want to know is, why did Sean quit school? His narrative simply states a family obligation."

Weir explained that Sean's mother, his only living relative, had been diagnosed with terminal breast cancer, and Sean had left school to care for her. He returned to school after her death. "He takes his obligations seriously," the professor went on. "He didn't elaborate in the narrative because Sean is a very private person and is not the type to casually discuss the death of his mother as part of an application." He went on to defend Sean's grades and his work ethic, but again Coleman cut him off. Weir wasn't telling him anything he didn't already know.

"What about his father?" Coleman asked.

"Sean has no contact with his father. He left him and his mother for another woman when Sean was just a baby. It is my understanding that he has never seen his father and has no desire to ever see him."

Coleman finished the conversation quickly because he suddenly felt uncomfortable discussing Sean with the good professor. It was strange; he wondered if the professor had more than just professorial interest in the young man.

"THIS luncheon…. Are we required to attend?" Sean didn't want to go and really couldn't imagine that Coleman would want either him or Ed there.

"I won't be going," Ed said. "Unfortunately I've already made arrangements to finish the Carlson depositions at city hall on Friday at one. I can't postpone it; it was a bear to arrange as it was." He patted Sean's arm as he got up from the desk. "I'll leave it up to you whether you go or not. I understand how you must feel." He stopped at the doorway and turned back as if he'd suddenly remembered something. "I do believe that Coleman wants you there."

"I doubt that," Sean said sarcastically.

"He invited you personally and even reiterated the invitation after he knew who you were." Ed rubbed his chin absently. "He would like to have you there, but I'll leave the decision up to you."

"I'm not going," Sean said to himself after Ed had left the room. "Especially not alone. No way, no how," he continued to mumble.

Sean was apprehensive the next day, still waiting for the hammer to come down on him, but nothing happened. He went about his day as before. He couldn't imagine Coleman would just let it go. He was not a man who allowed anyone to take advantage of him. There was no way they would simply allow Sean to continue his internship here after he'd specifically rejected him. Sean waited for Coleman to turn on him; he knew it was just a matter of time.

Friday around one thirty, Sean made sure he was out of the way. He didn't want to attend the lunch but also didn't want to be seen avoiding it. Sean hid out in the first-floor law library, pretending to be engrossed in his research. He was fairly confident no one would look for him there. It was best to stay out of sight and keep a low profile with regard to Coleman. Out of sight was out of mind (or at least he could hope).

It was just past one forty-five when he heard someone enter the library. He looked up, expecting one of the lowly researchers like himself, but instead his gaze was caught and held by none other than Coleman himself, who was casually striding toward him. A wave of tense apprehension washed over him, and he stiffened noticeably in his seat. Sean's first thought was that he was coming to tell him to get out. Coleman came around to his side of the table, seated himself on the edge, and crossed his arms, just inches from Sean's left arm. He was dressed in his usual immaculate black suit. Sean froze and waited for him to speak.

"Why aren't you at the luncheon?"

Not what he had expected. It took him a moment to process what Coleman had just said. Sean said the only thing that came to his mind at that moment: "What?" Having him so close was causing him to shake slightly. Sean grabbed hold of the book he was reading even tighter in an attempt to control his hands.

"The luncheon has begun. Why aren't you there?" Coleman smiled at him.

Sean continued to stare, wondering why he was being so nice. Why did he want him there? Was he going to publicly humiliate him during lunch? Was he going to make an example out of him and have security remove him from the premises during the lunch?

"Mr. Murray had to leave, and I didn't want to go by myself." It was the only excuse his feeble mind could come up with.

Coleman stood up abruptly and said, "Come. I'll be your escort." Coleman could feel Sean's anxiety and distrust. "Don't be afraid."

His words were warm and strangely comforting. Sean stood slowly and obediently followed him to the elevator in silence. Coleman reached out and directed Sean into the elevator with a gentle hand on the small of his back. He pushed the button for the eighth floor, and Sean noticed that he left his hand on his back throughout the ride. He wasn't sure what it meant; it had a comforting feel to it in the way Coleman's thumb moved in a circular pattern on his lower back muscle. But it had to be a controlling gesture, a way to show him he was going regardless of whether he wanted to.

Neither spoke, but much was communicated. When the elevator doors opened, Coleman dropped his hand from Sean's back and took his hand in a firm grip. This was about control, no doubt about it. Coleman began to exit the elevator but stopped when he realized Sean wasn't moving. A paralyzing apprehension enveloped him and he couldn't seem to get his legs to move. *This is ridiculous,* he thought as he frantically tried to move. What was causing this? Was it Coleman? Was it the eighth floor? Or was it fear of showing his face at the luncheon, knowing the other interns knew he had been rejected by this firm?

Coleman stopped the elevator doors, and they stood there together in silence for a while longer. "What's wrong Sean?" His voice was soft as silk.

"What are you going to do to me? Why are you insisting I be at this luncheon?" Sean tried to ease his hand away, but Coleman tightened his grip. *He's not going to release me,* Sean thought.

"I'm sorry," Coleman stated very clearly. He gripped Sean's hand even tighter and let his gaze travel Sean's face, searching for understanding, perhaps. "I am sorry for rejecting your application. You deserve to be at this luncheon; I want you to be there." What Coleman didn't tell him was that he'd arranged the entire event for him. It was simply a vehicle for him to meet Sean. He had never had a luncheon for interns in the past, but Sean didn't need to know that.

Sean ultimately relented and slowly exited the elevator. It felt uncomfortable being on the eighth floor, knowing he had been considered unsuitable for placement there. Coleman held his arm as they walked the long hallway toward what he assumed was a dining area. Sean garnered a lot of attention as people saw them together and realized he was attending the luncheon with Coleman as his escort. Every head turned in astonishment when they entered the room with Coleman holding firmly to his upper arm.

The partners who had interns knew how Coleman felt about this particular student and had been dumbfounded by his behavior over the past couple of days. When they found out that Ed's intern was none other than Sean Robbins, the intern Coleman had so vocally rejected, it was expected that both he and Ed would be out. Coleman wasn't accustomed to being disregarded. Ed had gone directly against his wishes when he accepted Sean, and he knew the consequences. No one felt bad for Ed, because he knew what he was doing, but most did feel sorry for Sean. Coleman had branded him an undesirable based on a hastily read application. Sean had obviously strived to rise above his lot in life only to see his future heartlessly derailed by Coleman West and Associates. Only Ed had had the integrity to treat him right, even if it hadn't been the most popular course of action.

They watched Coleman lead Sean to the long table and seat him next to himself. He held his hand and looked at him with an expression that was both friendly and admiring.

Sean was cautious as he looked around the room, hoping not to make eye contact with Brittany. There were more interns there than Sean had expected. He saw the four girls from his class. He felt the glare of Brittany Saunders. She was seated next to an older woman rather than next to Coleman. All the other interns were seated next to their supervisors. Sean wondered if Brittany had proved too common and, like him, had been rejected.

Coleman sat down next to him and seemed to be awfully close. Sean tried to adjust his chair to give Coleman more room, but Coleman adjusted as well, moving nearer again. Sean wasn't sure what it meant, but he knew he could not move away any further without annoying the man next to him.

The lunch itself was light but elegant. Sean found himself unable to eat, so he pushed his food around on his plate in an attempt to make it look as if he'd eaten. The whole time his entire awareness was focused on the man seated next to him. He was waiting for the ax to fall. He was waiting for the laughter and the security man to haul him out of the room and out of the building.

Coleman spoke softly to Sean, wanting to get to know more about him and about his placement experience so far. He leaned into Sean as if listening closely to him, but actually used it as an excuse to just get closer. Sean smelled wonderful: his hair, his skin, and his clothing all possessed an aroma that was nearly intoxicating. Coleman found himself breathing deeply and moving closer still. He moved one hand, letting it drape across the back of Sean's chair, and turned nearly completely into him, ignoring everyone else at the table.

All of the interns received gold associate's pins and certificates of placement. Everyone seemed excited with their little tokens of achievement. All except for Sean; they held no value for him. He didn't see himself as a Coleman West and Associates intern. He had been rejected, and he wouldn't be here if it weren't for the kindness of Professor Weir and Edward Murray. These tokens were not for him—they belonged to real interns. He toyed with them and then set them aside as if they didn't really belong to him.

Coleman gave a short speech of encouragement and success, and mentioned the dangers of prejudice and biased thinking. Sean thought him the biggest of hypocrites at that moment. The man had written the book on bias and prejudice, and still he had the nerve to preach.

As soon as the function looked to be breaking up, Sean made a hurried exit, avoiding and dodging everyone who attempted to catch him up in conversation. He wanted out. He wanted to go back to Ed's office, where he felt safe and accepted. On his way to the elevator, he took the certificate and with one hand crumpled it and tossed it and the pin into the trash next to the elevator. He was unaware that Coleman was watching him closely from the moment he made his dash for the door until he disappeared into the elevator.

Ed was in the office when Sean finally made it back. "How was it?" he greeted him with a big smile. "I heard that West himself came for you. Is that true?"

"It's true," Sean stated very seriously. "I don't know why, but he personally escorted me to this lunch."

"I don't know why either, Sean." Ed was about to turn back to his desk, and then suddenly swung around to face him with a look of concern. "Be careful. Coleman... he doesn't tolerate insubordination. He can be... cruel." He was still staring at Sean and then reiterated, "Be careful, son." He then went back to his desk and the papers he was reviewing.

Sean was silent for the remainder of the day. Having Ed voice his concerns was disconcerting enough. It was a given that Coleman would ultimately make an example out of him in some form or fashion. He realized being kicked out would be minor compared to the total devastation Coleman could bring down on him as far as his career was concerned. He could see to it that Sean never worked a day in the legal field—he had that kind of power. Sean knew he was good, and he didn't want to have to change careers simply because Coleman decided he was unworthy. He was contemplating which state he could relocate to that might not have heard of Coleman when there was a knock on his door. *That's strange*, he thought, *Ed never knocks*. But he didn't contemplate that thought too long; he simply stated, "Come in." To his surprise and shock, Coleman strode casually in and closed the door behind him. *This is it*, Sean thought, *he's going to sack me*. Coleman reached out to him and Sean jerked back.

"I'm sorry," Coleman said as his gaze searched Sean's face, reading everything.

Sean didn't respond. He had nothing to say. He backed up until he was flat against the bookcase that stood against the back wall. Finally, he pulled himself together and began to gather his belongings. He took his messenger bag and started to empty his desk of his books, reference materials, etcetera.

"What are you doing?"

Sean looked at him and saw that he was smiling. *Wow, that is cold*, he thought as he answered very quietly, "I'm leaving. Isn't that why you're here? To see me off of the premises?"

"Certainly not," Coleman stated as he took the bag from his shoulder and set it aside.

Sean noticed that his hand was gentle and warm as it brushed his shoulder.

"I realize that it is Friday night and you probably have other plans, but I'm going to make a request of you anyway."

Sean had difficulty focusing on what he was saying. It wasn't making any sense to him. He was still certain Coleman was going to kick him out. He wasn't kind and he wasn't friendly, so there had to be more to it.

"I have a business dinner at six, and my secretary is unable to accompany me. I need someone to record the meeting. Will you come?" Coleman spoke casually and actually looked sincere.

"What?" This was not what Sean had expected at all. What did he mean, record a meeting? Come to a business dinner with him? *What?*

Coleman saw the confusion and the distrust in his expression. He smiled and laid a hand on his arm, hoping to relax him, but which resulted in the opposite. "I would appreciate it if you would assist me this evening. It will be a good experience for you," he added.

"You want… me?" Sean managed to stutter it out.

"Yes, I want you." If those words had been said by anyone else the way he had just said them, Sean would have taken them as a seductive come-on. But Coleman was definitely not interested in him, not in that way.

Before he could reply, Coleman turned away, saying, "I'll collect you at five thirty here. If that's okay?" He paused, then added with a strange look of concern on his face, "You can meet me at my office if you'd prefer."

"No," Sean said too quickly. "Here is good." Coleman continued to stare at him as if he were going to say more, but instead turned and left the office, then closed the door gently behind him.

Sean waited for a while to make sure Coleman was gone. He stepped out to see Ed standing at the doorway to his office, staring at the hallway exit.

He heard Sean and turned to regard him with surprise. "You're working with Coleman this evening?"

Was it a question or a statement? Sean wasn't sure. "I guess so," he said lamely. "Why would he ask me to be his secretary for this function?"

Ed couldn't help him with any kind of answer. He was thinking that perhaps Coleman wasn't the narrow-minded bastard everyone thought he was, or maybe... no, he didn't want to think of the many ways Coleman could make Sean suffer if he chose to. "Maybe he has recognized your skill, just as I told you," Ed answered after too long of a pause.

Sean considered his statement for a moment but ended up shaking his head. "I doubt that has happened." He smiled weakly.

"If you have any... problems... if you need help, call me. I'll be home all evening. Call me, and I will come and get you." That was the nicest thing anyone had ever said to Sean. It touched him that Mr. Murray was willing to risk so much for him.

"I'll be fine. If it turns sour, I'll catch a cab. Don't worry," Sean reassured him.

THREE

ED LEFT just after 5:00 p.m. Before he left, he reiterated to Sean to be very careful and to call if he needed help. He felt a strong paternal instinct with Sean. It wasn't because Sean was weak or helpless; it was more that Sean needed to have someone in his corner, someone on his side. He was near in age to his own three children, and Ed hoped that if any of them were in need, someone would step up and help them.

Sean was on pins and needles as he waited for Coleman to appear. Before he arrived, Sean decided he would treat him like any other boss he had had. He would put out of his mind the fact that he despised him and would get through this evening with grace if not pride. Whatever Coleman had planned, Sean would handle it. He coached himself softly until he heard the elevator stop and a set of heavy, determined footsteps headed in his direction.

"Good, you're ready." Coleman took him by the hand and swiftly led him to the elevator and down to his car in the parking garage. This was the second time today that he'd taken his hand and held it while they walked together. Sean had never noticed him doing this with anyone else, male or female, and he wasn't sure what to make of it. He assumed it had something to do with showing his power and control.

Sean hesitated slightly before he opened his door and got in.

Coleman didn't seem to notice, or so Sean thought, but unbeknownst to Sean, Coleman had noticed. He noticed everything about Sean. "You're very quiet," he commented after they'd been driving for about ten minutes.

"Why am I here?" Sean asked bluntly. "You rejected my application; you refused to work with me. Why am I here?"

Coleman could hear the edge in Sean's voice. "You're here because I misjudged you," Coleman answered more calmly than he was feeling. "You should have had the placement you applied for; I'm sorry." He turned to look at Sean, but he was looking out his side window. Coleman wasn't sure if he believed him or not. "You don't like me very much, do you, Sean?" he asked suddenly.

Sean turned to him, caught his gaze, and held it. "I don't like you at all," he stated candidly.

"Because I rejected your application?"

"No, because of the things you wrote."

It became clear to Coleman that Sean had read the rejection letter he had sent to Professor Weir. It was unusual and rather unkind for an instructor to share such a negative correspondence with a student. "Did Professor Weir give you the letter?" He wanted to know if Weir was that unkind.

"No, I saw the envelope on his desk the day he told me I was rejected." Sean saw no reason to deny his actions. "When he left the office for something, I took the letter and replaced the envelope. He never knew I took it."

"Do you still have it?"

"Yes."

"Why?"

"It gives me perspective." Sean turned to stare, once again, out the passenger window. They both fell into a tense silence that lasted until they arrived at their destination. Coleman graciously held Sean's door for him as he got out and then took his arm, as if he were his date or something equally intimate, rather than just his personal assistant. A part of Sean reveled in the attention he was getting from everyone in the room. He detected envy in more than one stare. If they knew the truth, he thought, they wouldn't envy him. Pity, maybe, but not envy. He stiffened slightly as they entered the hotel ballroom.

"You'll be fine, Sean," Coleman said to him supportively and squeezed his arm a little tighter. He smiled down at him with a warmth and friendliness that took Sean by surprise.

Sean looked up at him and said, "Yes, sir." He didn't trust this man, not for a moment. Coleman's statement that he had misjudged him and was sorry sounded good and probably would have been enough for someone who hadn't had the lifelong disappointments Sean had had. Sorry was a very easy word to say and it usually meant nothing. Sorry was for the benefit of the deliverer, not the recipient.

Coleman got Sean a glass of wine and one for himself. Sean stared at the liquid for a few minutes before deciding to drink it very slowly.

Coleman watched Sean very closely, taking in every nuance of attitude, expression, and stance. A business associate cornered him and started discussing something. The best Coleman could do was nod; his thoughts were focused on and consumed by the intriguing young man he'd brought with him. *How could I be so cruel?* Coleman was thinking. *Why did I judge him so harshly without ever having laid eyes on him?* Many questions were rushing through his thoughts as he continued to watch him. Sean hated him; he knew that much for sure. He'd said so in the car. He hated him for the things that he had written. He saw Coleman as a self-righteous bastard with the power to ruin his career, and therefore he was forced to put up with him. If only… damn, those were the two most pathetic words in the English language. He turned his attention to the man speaking and tried to catch up with the conversation.

Sean was feeling very out of place. Dinner meeting, Coleman had said. This was a dinner party; a party he really felt did not include him. Slowly, he made his way over to one of the windows. Coleman was preoccupied with the lawyer from Detroit, so he didn't notice him slipping away, or so he thought. The crowd was centralized in the main hall. The window on the south side was far away from the flow of traffic and networking. It was secluded and quiet. If Coleman needed him, he would have to come and find him. No way was he going to follow him around like a puppy dog all night.

One of the catering staff came up to him and offered him some sort of cracker, pâté thing that he wasn't completely familiar with, but as he was hungry, eagerly accepted.

"Sean?" the waitress asked.

Sean looked at her squarely and smiled broadly. "Francine," he said, delighted to see a friendly face. Sean and Francine had been classmates.

"What are you doing here?" she asked and handed Sean more crackers so she wouldn't look like she was socializing on the caterer's time.

"I'm here with Mr. Coleman West," he said between crackers.

"As his date?" Francine always jumped to the wrong conclusion.

"No, of course not! The man can barely tolerate me and my classlessness. He needed a secretary for the evening, and apparently I was the only one available."

"I'm pretty sure he could have found someone else if he wanted to. Men like Coleman West never have to settle. I've seen him at quite a few of these functions, and trust me, he doesn't lack for companionship."

"I'm just here as his assistant," Sean clarified.

"He's never needed an assistant here before." Francine was going to argue the point but was cut off.

"There you are, Sean." Coleman approached them both. "I thought I'd lost you." He smiled at Francine, who quickly turned to offer a cracker to another guest.

"I was just trying to stay out of the way," Sean said, and then he fell into step with Coleman as he was ushered to one of the large dinner tables. Coleman included Sean in his conversations and asked his opinions as if his views mattered. Coleman treated him like an equal, introducing Sean as one of his paralegals and not as the rejected university intern that he was. During dinner, Coleman sat close to him, and whenever Sean glanced in his direction, he saw him watching, studying him, almost. So intense was his scrutiny that at one point Sean asked softly through clenched teeth, "What am I doing wrong? Am I using the wrong fork, eating too fast, what is it?"

"Nothing is wrong," Coleman assured him. "You are absolutely perfect."

"Yes, a perfect reject," Sean muttered sarcastically.

"No, a perfect companion," Coleman stated clearly. Sean noticed he was not smiling and his eyes were dark and drawn. He'd angered him. He looked irritated. Sean knew when to shut up, and that time was now.

"Thank you, sir," he said softly without looking at him again. Sean had to admit to himself that Coleman was a very compelling man. No wonder he had a large, successful law firm at the age of thirty-two. He was clear, concise, strong, unyielding, and astutely intelligent. Sean ran these qualities through his mind and at the same time thought about his less attractive characteristics, such as: judgmental, rude, superior, and an insufferable snob. He had nothing in common with this man. Why he wanted him here was still a mystery. He said he needed someone to record the meeting, yet there was no meeting. There was nothing to record. This was simply a high-class dinner party put on by the local bankers trust.

It was nearly 10:00 p.m. when they left. Coleman made no mention of the fact that Sean really hadn't been needed at this party. If Sean didn't know better, he would have believed Coleman made up the whole story just to take him out, but that couldn't be the case. As Francine had pointed out, Coleman was never at a loss for companionship. *He certainly doesn't need to add my sorry ass to his entourage.* Sean smiled at his own thoughts.

"You should do that more often," Coleman said, joking, but with sincerity.

"What?"

"Smile. You have a beautiful smile, Sean." Sean didn't respond. They were soon in Coleman's car and on their way. Sean offered to get a cab so Coleman wouldn't have to drive him home, but the look he'd given Sean told him clearly not to suggest such a thing again.

"Why don't you smile more often?" he asked Sean after several minutes of silence.

"I do smile," Sean said.

"Just not around me, is that it?" he asked and again, Sean didn't respond for fear of offending him if he told him the truth.

"Mr. Murray makes me smile. He has a great sense of humor."

"You like Ed a lot?" Sean smiled the minute he said Ed's name, and it bothered Coleman.

"I love Ed Murray," Sean stated emphatically. "There isn't anything I wouldn't do for the man." Sean was oblivious to the effect his statement was having on Coleman.

Coleman didn't speak for some time after Sean's declaration about Ed. He was surprised by the feeling of jealousy overtaking him. He couldn't recall the last time he'd felt this degree of jealousy. He'd coveted many things in his life, but never the love and respect of another human being. Ed gave Sean a chance and a sense of equality, and for that he got undying loyalty. If only.... Damn, he hated those words.

Coleman pulled into an apartment complex and asked Sean, "Which building is your apartment in, building one or two?"

Sean was confused and didn't have a clue why Coleman thought he lived in one of these buildings. No way could he afford this kind of rent. "I don't live here," he stated, and then i was Coleman's turn to be confused.

"All Coleman West and Associates interns live here. You're given an apartment when you're given a placement," he said.

"I wasn't given a placement," Sean answered softly. "I'm not a Coleman West and Associates intern; I'm Ed Murray's intern. I don't live here."

Clarity hit Coleman as did the combined feeling of guilt and remorse.

"Where do you live?" he asked, his voice almost a whisper.

"On the south side, at the corner of Mitchell and 4th."

Coleman knew the area. It was a low-rent, run-down section of town. He clenched his teeth and his expression hardened.

Sean saw the change in him and assumed it was due to his frustration at having to drive him to another location. "You can let me out here," he suggested in a harsh tone. "I can call a cab." He was attempting to get out of the car when Coleman grabbed him by the arm and demanded he stay in the car.

"What the hell are you doing?" Coleman cursed.

"I can find my own way home. I don't need your help," Sean shot back.

Coleman threw the car into park and turned on him. "I'm driving you home. I know you hate me. I know you'd rather be anywhere than in this car with me, but it's not safe to be on these streets alone at this time of night. So suck up your pride and let me drive you home." His eyes were dark and serious, and his anger was evident in the tight expression of his body. Sean decided it would be a good idea to agree with him. He nodded his acceptance and turned away to look out the side window so he wouldn't have to let him see that he'd won.

Coleman brought the shiny black car to a stop in front of Sean's run-down apartment building.

"I don't hate you, Mr. West," Sean said offhandedly. "I don't like you, that's for certain." He smiled weakly. "But I don't know you well enough to hate you. Perhaps that will come later," he added with a bigger smile and a laugh.

"God, I hope not," Coleman answered and also laughed, but there was also a hint of desperation in his words. "I want you to know me better, but I don't want you to hate me," he clarified. His mood seemed suddenly lighter, happier, as if Sean not hating him actually meant something. "I'll walk you to your door," he said as he exited the car and waited for Sean. They walked together up the flight of rickety stairs to Sean's apartment door. The other two apartments on the second floor were larger than his and held two persons each. Sean's apartment was barely larger than a walk-in closet, but it was all he could afford. He could tell by the look on Coleman's face as he surveyed the area that he was far from impressed.

Sean unlocked his door and was about to thank him and say good night, when Coleman quickly stepped into his apartment and closed the door behind him. Sean stared in disbelief at his forwardness and was about to demand that he leave immediately.

Coleman smiled, sensing the direction of his thoughts and said casually but firmly, "I'll search your apartment before I leave. Your door is far from secure, and someone could have easily gotten in here while you were out. This neighborhood is notorious for break-ins." Without waiting for Sean to approve, he surveyed the combination living room and kitchen and checked the one closet. Coleman then proceeded to Sean's bedroom, which was just big enough for a twin-size bed. He got down on one knee and checked under the bed. Coleman finished with the bathroom and even looked in the shower stall, in case someone might have been hiding behind the curtain.

Sean followed him at a distance, a part of him concerned that perhaps he would find an intruder and might need his help When Coleman finished, he returned to the living room. He said nothing but stood there as if contemplating something.

Probably not the posh digs he was used to, Sean thought, but too bad; it was the best that he could do, and besides, Coleman didn't have to live there, so why did he care?

Coleman was about to speak when they heard a loud knock on the door. Without asking, he threw open the door and towered malevolently over the stout young man who stood there, obviously intoxicated and just as obviously taken aback by the larger man's presence.

"What do you want?" he barked at him.

"We're having a party," the young man stammered. "I thought the guy who lives here might want to come." He paused for a second and then added, "Do you live here?"

Coleman eyed him with anger. "Yes, I do! And the guy who lives here is not interested in attending your party!" As he slammed the door, he finished with, "Don't come here again!"

Sean stood there, unable to respond. What was he, his keeper? he thought, irritated with the way Coleman seemed to have taken over.

Coleman turned on him then and, pointing an angry finger at him, stated, "You're not staying here tonight."

"What?" he said curtly.

"You're not safe here. A party, intoxicated men, and a flimsy door do not equal safety."

"This is where I live," Sean said with conviction. "I can take care of myself; I've done so for years."

"You're a small-town guy. You're not familiar with what happens in a town like this one. You're not safe here." Coleman walked over to him. His presence, his height, his demeanor, his black suit, and his black stare were all intimidating. "You have two choices, Sean. You can pack a bag and stay in my guest room tonight, or I will sleep here on your sofa. I'm not leaving you here alone."

Sean recognized that he was completely serious, but neither choice sounded particularly attractive. "I'll be fine," he insisted. "I've lived here for nearly six weeks. I've had very few problems. If there is trouble, I'll call the police."

Coleman knew how quickly the police responded to this section of town, so he was far from convinced. "You have two choices," he repeated.

Sean looked at his lumpy sofa and figured the man would be hurting by morning if he had to sleep on that thing. Coleman followed his gaze and his train of thought.

"You're right," he said. "Not a very comfortable prospect."

Sean considered a motel room, but there was no way he could afford it.

"Get your bag," Coleman stated. "Bring everything that's important to you." He added thoughtfully, "I have a bad feeling about your neighbors and their party."

Sean hadn't brought much with him when he moved here for his internship, so packing was easily accomplished in a few minutes with one bag and a case for his sketches and few art projects he brought with him. On their way down, they met several people who were coming for the party, and all of them looked as if the party had started for them hours earlier. No one bothered them or even spoke. Coleman had a presence about him that made people back off. Sean was just as glad, because he wasn't in the mood to deal with drunks.

Sean was surprised when Coleman drove out of town and out into the secluded countryside. He had expected him to live in some gated community or a high-rise apartment. They drove for many miles before he turned onto a narrow drive that led to a huge estate nestled in the woods. Sean had pictured Coleman as a social-function magnet who attended all parties worth attending. This stately home painted an entirely different picture. The driveway and front of the house were illuminated with subtle amber lighting. Sean refused to show that he was impressed with what he saw. No need to stroke the man's ego any more than necessary. He knew he had a beautiful home; he didn't need Sean telling him so. They walked up a long, softly-lit stone walkway up to the large, arching front door of the house. Sean was very impressed by the sight.

Coleman explained that he'd bought the place three years earlier. He had an apartment in town, but he always escaped out here on the weekends. The home was three stories of stone and wood. It had been built at the turn of the century and had been well maintained over the years.

Sean was awed by the beautiful, intricate stone fireplace and the woodworking of the staircase and archways. Finally, he couldn't stand it any longer and expressed his appreciation of the workmanship of this home. "This fireplace is amazing." He sighed and walked over to it, running his hands over the stone. "Who made this?"

"R.F. Woodrow." Coleman pointed near the floor where the craftsman had signed. "His work is well known in this area," he added.

"It should be," Sean commented.

Coleman moved to stand close to Sean, impressed with his appreciation of the work of R.F. Woodrow. His gaze traveled Sean's face, taking in every emotion shown. This man was capable of deep, everlasting, all-consuming emotion. Coleman considered this thought for quite some time before backing away and showing him to his room.

He took Sean to a large bedroom on the second floor. Before leaving he said, "Make yourself comfortable and treat it like your own home."

Once he was gone, Sean sat down on the end of the bed and hugged his bag to his side. He was far from being comfortable. This wasn't his home. For all of his kindness and consideration tonight, Coleman was still the same man who wrote that hateful letter. The same man who had no qualms about ruining his career before it even started. Sean sat on the bed and stared at the floor. The large wooden clock on the bedside table read 12:15 a.m. Sean watched the minutes tick by. He was startled to awareness by a gentle knock on his door. He realized the clock now read 1:10 a.m. and he was still dressed and sitting on the end of the bed.

The door opened slowly and Coleman walked into the room. He saw that Sean hadn't moved, hadn't lain down. He sat there, fully dressed with his bag next to him, as if waiting for the next bus.

"I saw your light on," he said as he approached Sean. "I thought perhaps you were having some difficulty sleeping." Coleman paused as he came to stand directly in front of him. "I didn't realize you were having this much difficulty."

Sean looked up at him. Coleman was wearing pajama bottoms and no top. His chest was tanned and muscled and covered with a thin layer of dark hair. Sean averted his gaze. He felt the urge to stare, a desire to reach out and run his fingertips down the center of Coleman's chest, following the flow of the silken hair and feel the juncture of the muscles. He blushed and stared resolutely at the floor. Sure, Coleman was physically attractive, he told himself, but there was nothing under the skin that he was the least bit attracted to.

"Are you going to sit there like that for the entire night? You could at least take your shoes off." Coleman sat down next to him. "Why are you afraid to go to sleep?"

"I'm not afraid. I just don't feel right being here."

"Would it help if I made you a cup of tea or some hot milk?" Coleman asked as he gently removed Sean's suit coat, took his bag from his grasp, and set them both to one side.

Oh great, Sean thought. *Now he's going to treat me like an infant.* "No, thank you. I'll be fine. What time can I leave in the morning?"

"Is the thought of staying here tonight really this distasteful for you?" Coleman got up, dropped down on one knee in front of him, and silently began unlacing his shoe. He was undressing him. Coleman encircled his ankle with his hand as he removed Sean's right shoe. It took every bit of his self-control not to jerk his foot away. Coleman then took off his left shoe and began a slow massage of his foot, pinning him with his gaze while he massaged and soothed Sean with his hands. It was sensuous and it was delicious. Parts of Sean's body better left ignored began to spring to life, tingling and needy. How was it that his body wanted Coleman, while his mind disliked and distrusted him? His second thought was that no one would believe Coleman West was on his knees in front of him, massaging his foot. "I'll fix you a cup of tea," Coleman said at last, softly but firmly. "When I return, you had better be undressed and in bed, or I will do the honors. Understood?"

"Understood," Sean answered. Coleman's expression left no doubt that he would carry out his threat.

Before Coleman left the room, he asked, "Is it really that bad?"

"Yes," Sean answered. As soon as the door closed, Sean quickly undressed and got into bed. He didn't want to test Coleman on this score. If he started to undress him, Sean probably wouldn't stop him. He knew enough about what he was feeling to know that he wanted him… only physically, of course, he assured himself.

"Good," Coleman said as he entered his room a short time later with a cup of tea. "Now drink this and go to sleep." He handed him the cup and his hand touched Sean's. He didn't immediately let go of the cup, and instead took in the blush and the way Sean averted his eyes.

"I'm sorry," Coleman said remorsefully. "I'm sorry. I can't undo what's already done. But I would like to try and make amends if you will let me." He sat down and leaned into him with his left arm draped across Sean's legs, which were under the comforter.

"Why?" Sean asked and placed the cup of tea on the bedside table. "I'm the same person I was two months ago. The same person you researched and deemed unsuitable. I'm still low class, ill-bred, and worthless; I haven't changed."

"I've changed," Coleman said curtly. "And you aren't and never were any of those things." He raised his right hand to gently caress Sean's cheek, running his fingers across the smooth feel of his skin as he pleaded with his gaze. Slowly, he leaned closer and gradually pulled Sean into the circle of his arms. He then drew Sean up firmly against him.

Sean did not resist. He could feel the muscle definition of Coleman's bare arms and chest through the thin T-shirt he was wearing. His kiss was hypnotic and better than any Sean had experienced so far. The moment Coleman's lips touched him, they ignited a need from the very depths of his being. This was a need that ached for physical satisfaction. Coleman tasted like power and heat. Sean fought the urge to raise his hand, caress his cheek, and run his fingers through the silkiness of his hair. Coleman's release was also slow, his gaze never leaving Sean's. He seemed to be testing him to gauge Sean's reaction and his acceptance.

Sean pulled back from him abruptly, suddenly embarrassed and off-balance. Coleman maintained his gentle but firm grip on his upper arms. "Why did you do that?" Sean asked. "That's hardly appropriate behavior with one's intern," he said sharply.

"As you have never tired of reminding me, you are not my intern," Coleman answered casually with a smile. Sean did not respond, just lowered his eyes to stare down at the comforter covering him to his waist. "It's okay," Coleman assured him softly. "You're safe here. I haven't raped anyone in years," he added sarcastically, and Sean took immediate offense.

"I'm not worried," Sean shot back icily. "I'm hardly your type. You've made that abundantly clear."

"Don't push me, Sean," Coleman warned with a sultry stare. "I might be tempted to give you a demonstration to show how wrong you are." He reached up and smoothed Sean's hair back from his face. His touch was like a narcotic. Sean just wanted more. Holding his hand, touching his back, and smoothing his hair had become common behavior for Coleman when it came to Sean. Sean was beginning to crave his touch, leaning into it and lingering longer than necessary. He found his touch invigorating and he didn't know why. Perhaps his excitement stemmed from the novelty of having someone like Coleman appear interested in touching him. Whatever it was, Sean desperately wanted to reach out and take Coleman's hand, but through sheer force of will held his hands in two tight fists at his sides in order to maintain control.

"I'm tired," Sean declared in an attempt to end the conversation and the contact.

"I'll say good night, then." Coleman did not protest his obvious attempt to escape. "My room is next door. If you need anything during the night, don't hesitate to wake me."

"Thank you," Sean said and looked up at him to see if he was still making fun of him, but he wasn't; he looked serious. "Thank you," Sean repeated, warmer and more genuine.

FOUR

SEAN slept sporadically throughout the night. It was impossible for him to completely relax. He couldn't wait for morning and the chance to get away from Coleman. He thought hard on the events of the day and for the life of him couldn't figure out what Coleman was planning. Did he really have a conscience? Did he feel bad for dismissing Sean's application? He had been warned by many that Coleman did not tolerate insubordination and that he was neither kind nor forgiving. Ed had gone against his wishes and behind his back to accept Sean. That was not something he was just going to let go. Ed had told him to be careful and that was exactly what he planned to be.

As soon as he saw the first sign of morning through his window, Sean was out of bed and in the shower. Usually on Saturday, he would sleep in till 9:00 or 10:00 a.m., but this was no normal Saturday. Perhaps he could call a cab. His cell phone didn't show a signal, so Sean decided to look for a house phone. Coleman might be still asleep and not ready or willing to drive him home. He could only hope.

Sean was showered, dressed, and downstairs by 6:00 a.m. He moved quietly for fear of disturbing Coleman. He found the telephone next to the hall lamp, between the living room and the kitchen. He could make his call, write a note explaining that he'd left, and thank Coleman for his hospitality. A rush of relief washed over him as he reached for the phone, but it was replaced by startled shock when Coleman stepped out of the kitchen.

"Good morning, Sean." He smiled and handed him a cup of coffee. "I hope I didn't wake you." Sean shook his head and dropped his bag next to the small hall table. "Come," he directed while placing a gentle hand on the small of Sean's back. "Breakfast is ready. I was planning on serving you in bed, but since you're up, let's eat on the patio."

Sean followed obediently, his mind consumed with the statement that Coleman had planned to serve him breakfast in bed. His kindness, attentiveness, and consideration were now so over the top, Sean was certain it all had to be an act of some kind. Was he trying to put him at ease enough so that he would do something stupid? Something that would seal his character as the lowlife he labeled him? But why go to all this trouble? He could get satisfaction very easily. He was the boss; public humiliation and a prompt dismissal were within his power and he could do that at any time.

Coleman led Sean outside, to a patio garden off the kitchen, and seated him at a small, intimate table. He moved about quickly, setting the table and then serving a breakfast of omelet, toast, and coffee. Sean observed in silence. He seemed so comfortable and at ease with him. Mr. West was dressed very casually. Sean had only seen him in the seriously intimidating black suits, so his dark jeans and crew-neck sweater were a nice change. He looked more human, more approachable. He gave Sean a glass of orange juice and then seated himself directly across from him.

"Did you sleep well?" he asked politely. Sean looked at him directly, assessing the question and deciding his answer. The truth was no, but if he told the truth he would have to explain why, and then that would lead to probable interrogation and possible offense. It was easier to lie.

"Yes, very well, thank you," he answered.

Coleman laughed out loud. "I doubt that. I heard you tossing and turning all night."

"I slept fine," Sean persisted. *Can't admit to lying... must press forward and convince him I slept.*

Coleman simply smiled and went back to his meal. He wasn't convinced. As they were finishing, he proposed that perhaps Sean should move into the apartments supplied by the firm. He knew he was definitely on the wrong track when Sean didn't answer, but simply stared at him as if he were insane.

"Why not?" He countered without ever receiving an answer.

"The girls I had class with are there," Sean said clearly. "They know I did not receive a placement like theirs. I am fine where I am." He was firm on this point.

Coleman thought about it for a few moments and then realized Sean was concerned about what they would think. He was worried about his reputation. They would see it as a favor from the boss, instead of a sign of his competency. "Okay, I understand, but that apartment of yours is not acceptable."

"It is all that I can afford."

"Then I will have to increase your stipend."

"I don't receive a stipend."

"All interns receive a weekly stipend...." He trailed off as he remembered Sean was not his intern. He was Ed Murray's intern. "How do you support yourself?" He was truly interested.

"Mr. Murray pays me what he can, and I work part time at Lake View Janitorial Services." Sean hated having to explain himself. His finances were his own business. *Just let me go home!* he wanted to scream.

Coleman stood up and began to gather the dirty dishes. Sean also stood and tried to assist him, but Coleman told him to sit and relax. He was clearing the table simply because he needed time to think. How could he convince Sean to accept a stipend large enough to afford a decent place to live without offending him?

Sit and relax, Sean said to himself sarcastically. *I can sit, but relaxing is not in my power.* He wondered if he could bring up the subject of taking him home. He would offer to pay for a cab first. He checked his watch.

Coleman saw this as he continued clearing the table. He probably wanted to go home, but Coleman needed a reason for him to move out of that apartment. He had been living there for nearly six weeks. That thought brought with it severe pangs of guilt. That area was dangerous, and he would not have someone working at his firm living there. He didn't make him leave last night simply because he wanted to spend more time with him, which he had, but that wasn't the reason. Coleman knew Sean was in real danger last night; he felt it. He would not allow him to live there any longer. He understood Sean's hesitation in accepting one of the apartments offered by the firm. His schoolmates knew what had happened. They knew his application had not been accepted, and he didn't want to deal with their questions and speculations. Besides, Coleman didn't really want Sean living in one of the intern quarters. He wanted access to him; he wanted the freedom to see him without the prying eyes of the other interns. He finished cleaning and sat down again, facing Sean.

"May I call a cab, sir?" were Sean's first words.

"I will drive you home." Coleman watched him for a few moments before adding, "I want to offer you a stipend, like the other interns receive, so you won't have to work another job. I like my employees to stay focused on the one job when they work for me, and it will also help Ed. None of the other supervisors pay for their intern."

"I'm not one of your interns," Sean countered. He wanted nothing from him. He would take care of himself. He wanted no strings tying him to Coleman. "Stipends are for students whose applications were accepted. I simply work for Mr. Murray, and my professor is kind enough to count it towards internship hours. When I finish, I will receive a certificate signed by Mr. Edward Murray, P.C."

Coleman stared at him for several long silent minutes before speaking. "When you develop a grudge, you really hold onto it." There was a slight grin on his face but he tried to control it. Now was not the time to laugh. He'd never met a man so stubborn, so self-reliant, so adorable in his insistence to accept nothing from the likes of him. "You're getting a stipend and the check will read 'Coleman West and Associates'. You will use the money to rent a decent apartment and you will quit your part-time job." He was firm but tried not to be threatening. "I know you'd rather die than take anything from me, but you will take the money, understood?" Sean nodded but did not speak. "All I need is to have you end up injured or worse due to criminal activity at that fleabag apartment building. The first thing the papers would grab hold of is that you are an intern at my firm. The negative publicity would cost me more than the money I'm going to give you so you can live safely." He stood up and headed back inside, and Sean followed him. Sean had to agree that it made sense. He would accept simply because to refuse would probably mean dismissal.

Coleman grabbed his keys and together they walked out to his car. The first stop was Davis Realty, to check on available one-bedroom apartments near the firm. He didn't want Sean to have to walk too far. He knew it would be impossible to get him to agree to use a company car, so he didn't try. He got copies of several possibilities, and with a Realtor in tow, they were on their way again.

"This isn't necessary," Sean insisted. It seemed as though Coleman was trying to control his life. Telling him where to live, how to live, and who to live near. It infuriated him, but he had to stay calm. Coleman could do him and Ed a lot of damage if he chose to.

"Yes, it is necessary," Coleman responded offhandedly. His tone indicated that the subject was not open to discussion.

Coleman stole a glance at him. Sean was so proud, too proud for his own good. The only thing that would truly make Sean happy right now would be for Coleman to drive him home to that wretched apartment and drop him off. His discomfort filled the air between them. "You put in your application that you worked at a local nightclub. What did you do there?"

"It wasn't a nightclub. It was more of a local pub," he clarified. "I worked cleanup from 2:00 to 5:00 a.m. on the weekend." Sean then decided to clear the air a little. "I quit school in order to take care of my mother. She didn't want me to, but I had to know she was properly cared for, so it had to be me. I would not leave her in the hands of strangers." Sean turned to regard him squarely as Coleman continued to drive. "Is there anything else in my application that you would like clarification on?"

"Just one more item," Coleman stated, unaffected by Sean's demeanor. "Do you have any family?"

"No. I have friends and I have people who care about me, but I have no family left." He did not elaborate; he wasn't in the mood to explain his lack of family.

Sean was taken aback by the first apartment they looked at. It was located in one of the stately old buildings just off Michigan Avenue. It was a very upscale apartment building, and Sean could not envision himself actually living in such an environment of superiority and haughtiness.

"I'd prefer something small and out of the way." Sean voiced his opinion as they walked around the third town house-style apartment. Coleman looked at him once again, feeling his discomfort. Sean wasn't used to receiving financial assistance, and it was grating on him. Sean left the Realtor flipping through other possible apartments on a smaller scale. Coleman stood over Sean and pushed the hair back from his face with an ever-increasing familiarity. He let his hand linger and ran his fingers along Sean's jaw, causing him to naturally look up at him.

"I like this one. It's close to work and it's not very large," Coleman said. Coleman locked eyes with him, waiting for a reason why this was not going to work, but instead Sean nodded and turned away from him. Sean recognized the futility in arguing. Coleman respected Sean's sense of independence and his ability to take care of himself, but in this regard he had to accept help. If Sean wouldn't do it willingly, then Coleman was prepared to force the issue. He walked back over to the Realtor and began completing the paperwork.

Sean walked into the kitchen, away from the two men. They didn't need him. They were running his life just fine without any assistance from him. The kitchen was large and bright, with a window that gave a pleasant view of the courtyard. He admitted it would be nice to sit there in the morning and evening, watching the activity below while having a cup of coffee or tea. He only had one window in his other apartment, and it was in the bathroom. It looked out over a dilapidated garage that housed a three-legged dog and one junk car. This was definitely an improvement, but at what price?

Coleman came in to find him a while later. "Everything is set. You can move in immediately." He walked up behind him. Sean continued to stare out the window, but he was listening. Coleman ached to put his arms around his waist, bury his face in the crook of his neck, and drink in the freshness of him. Sean smelled like the air after a summer shower. He smelled heavenly. But Coleman refrained and simply put his hand on his arm. "I called a mover, and they will have your things here by this afternoon. You don't have to return to that apartment for anything."

Sean turned around to face him. Coleman adjusted his touch but maintained contact. "I appreciate what you are doing for me," he began, obviously struggling to put together the right words. "But you don't owe me anything. You are allowed your own opinions and judgments." Sean watched him, trying to discern any reaction, but Coleman was a master of control.

"I like you, Sean," Coleman said at last. "If I had met you before seeing your application, I guarantee you would have had a placement. No question." He let his hand drop down to grasp Sean's. "There are some horrid stories about me going around, and although some are based on truth, most are exaggerations. I'm not a bad person... really." He smiled and then laughed a self-deprecating laugh. "Let me help you—it will be good for my reputation."

Sean was somewhat taken aback. "I've heard many stories about you. But I also understand that someone in your position has to be tough, solid, even unyielding in your relationships with others. The stories did not define my opinion of you."

"No, my letter did that." Coleman looked almost embarrassed. "May I have the letter, please? I don't want you reading it and seeing that part of me over and over again." Coleman took another step toward Sean and continued to hold his hand, rubbing his palm with his thumb.

Sean considered the request for several minutes before reaching into his back pocket to get his wallet. Coleman let go of his hand but remained very close, almost looming over him. Sean opened his wallet, and tucked in behind several university cards and IDs was a folded piece of stationary. By the look of the stress on the creases, it had been folded and unfolded many times. He was about to unfold it when Coleman reached up and covered it with his hand.

"Don't read it, Sean." Coleman took the letter and crumpled it in his palm, holding it in a firm grip. "Thank you." He stuck the crumpled paper in the pocket of his jeans. He was so glad to have that insidious letter out of Sean's hands. When he had the opportunity, he planned on burning it. He never wanted it to be read ever again.

"How about lunch?" Without waiting for Sean to agree, Coleman took his hand and they started for the door. Before leaving, they stopped briefly to give the Realtor more instructions. Coleman held Sean's hand tightly until they reached the car, where he turned to regard Sean closely. Sean remained as disconnected as possible. He was unsure and distrustful and wasn't about to open up or speak with Coleman as an equal. Coleman wished he could get beyond this... beyond this fear and suspicion and get on with... he couldn't complete that thought. He wasn't sure what he wanted from Sean, but he knew for sure that he wanted to know him... better.

They had lunch at an outdoor café downtown. Coleman treated Sean like a treasured companion or close friend. Coleman was hard to understand and harder to disregard. Sean wanted to go home. He wanted time alone to process the past two days. How had his life gotten so far out of his own control?

"Tell me about yourself," Coleman stated after they'd finished their lunch and were enjoying a hot latte. "All I know is what I read in your application and the few snippets you've given." He watched Sean closely as he shifted nervously in his seat and glanced around the area, as if hoping for someone to save him from having to speak. Coleman could see his mind working as he tried to figure out what to say. He seemed guarded and unsure.

"I don't know what to say. What do you want to know?"

"Tell me about your childhood," Coleman began. "I don't think our childhoods were really that different, except I had money and you had a mother who gave a damn." He was speaking the truth and trying to put Sean at ease.

"I never knew my father." Sean looked at him squarely to gauge his response and saw only intensity in Coleman's eyes. "He left my mother when I was less than a year old. He found someone else and never looked back." Sean took a long sip of his latte in an attempt to buy some time. Sharing was not something he was comfortable with. Even his closest friends didn't know details of his life, but he felt an obligation to answer this man's questions, so he continued. "I don't know his name, and I have no interest in ever knowing. Robbins is my mother's name. She took it back after the divorce and changed mine at the same time. She supported me without any help from him, and after a period of no contact she petitioned the court to have his rights terminated. My mother had no family except for me, so she did it all on her own. She worked waitressing, and she worked at the library. She took almost any odd job she could get, and we had a good life together." Sean had a smile on his face when he finished. "My dream was to get a good job and take care of her for a change, but that didn't work out." His voice shook a little, and he shifted his gaze to his cup.

Coleman was touched by Sean's story, and by the obvious difficulty he had in sharing it. It was apparent that Sean didn't talk about himself much. He seemed to be more of a listener than a talker.

"My parents divorced when I was four," Coleman reciprocated. "They should have separated long before that, but my parents stayed together in order to irritate one another. My father had one affair after another and so did my mother. It was actually a blessing when they finally went their separate ways. The fighting was sometimes deafening and always hateful and ugly."

Sean was shocked by his admission. He remained quiet, waiting for him to continue. He had no idea Coleman had had anything less than the perfect childhood.

"I grew up in boarding schools. I saw my parents a couple of times a year. After I was past fifteen, I didn't see them except at their weddings, and they had many." Coleman did not avert his gaze, but held Sean's, waiting for a comment or a flicker of mocking interest, but he saw sincerity and care in his expression and in his silence. "I had some solid role models in my teachers and administrators. They gave me a place and they gave me a sense of importance when my performance warranted it. I believe that is why I have grown up to be so black and white in my opinions and judgments. My role models were stern and exacting. They taught me well. I'm not complaining—they gave me what I needed to survive without parental involvement in my life." He finally glanced away, taking a long sip of his latte.

Sean began, "I don't really know you, but you appear to handle yourself well, and it is obvious that you care about people. It isn't something that is overt, but if you pay attention, you see it." Sean smiled a genuine smile of warmth and connectedness that made Coleman melt inside. "You're a good man. You just don't want people to know it." This time he laughed, and Coleman joined him.

"Don't give away my secret," Coleman teased. "I've spent years making people afraid of me. I'd hate to think my time was wasted."

"Oh, you're fearsome all right. I spent a month running from you out of sheer dread." Sean stopped and took another sip, then drained the cup. He'd probably said too much, so he backed off into silence. He had begun to feel comfortable, therefore was stating his thoughts; not a good idea when dealing with someone like Coleman. He could turn on him... easily... and then what? *Time to shut up*, he told himself.

Coleman sensed the change immediately, and he wasn't going to tolerate it. "You don't have to fear me, Sean... ever." He reached out and took Sean's hand too aggressively. Sean winced but did not pull away. "I'm sorry," he stated and loosened his grip, but did not release him. "Tell me about your mother. What was it like to have someone who loved you unconditionally?" He wanted to get Sean talking again.

Sean unconsciously gripped Coleman's hand tighter as his mind traveled back to life spent with his mother. Coleman noticed and felt the depth of this man's devotion to his mother. Losing her must have devastated him. He had never experienced a connection like theirs, had never loved and been loved like Sean.

"I never doubted that I was the most important person in her life. There wasn't anything I couldn't discuss with her, and she always gave me the best advice. I trusted her completely. I miss her every single day," Sean ended with emphasis.

"I've never known anyone I have trusted completely." Coleman sounded almost forlorn as he continued to look at Sean. "I hope I do, someday."

"I hope you do too," Sean said softly. Coleman was about to say something more when a voice from their left intruded on their intimacy.

"Coleman, hey, how are you?" Sean recognized the person as one of the upper-level partners. His name was Jason Weintaub. Sean had expected Coleman to let go of his hand and to back off as soon as his coworker showed up, but he didn't. The man's presence prompted no change in Coleman's behavior.

"Hello," Coleman said, and he invited Jason to sit with them. He then introduced Jason to Sean. Jason was friendly and accepting of him, which Sean had not expected.

"So this is the mystery man," he said to Coleman laughingly.

"Yes, and he wasn't easy to find. Sean, here, knows how to hide." Coleman was laughing. Sean decided it must be an inside joke because he wasn't following the humor. Assuming their amusement was at his expense, Sean withdrew and waited for his opportunity to leave. He attempted to extract his hand from Coleman's grasp, but the other man wouldn't let him go.

Coleman immediately gave Sean his complete attention, read his discomfort, and apologized. "I'm sorry," he said gently. "Jason is the one who gave you up. He told me he thought you were Ed's intern when I described you to him. I wanted to know your name. I didn't understand why you were always running from me."

They continued to talk for a while about business and some personal issues, but Coleman recognized that Sean was aching to go home, so he finally relented, and they said their good-byes to Jason. He still held onto Sean's hand as they made their way to Coleman's car. It did not feel strange or awkward holding his hand.

That revelation confused Sean as he studied his feelings about the whole thing. Coleman's hand was strong and sure. The action made him feel… accepted… important… valued. He wasn't able to put an accurate label on the feeling, but it was a good, secure feeling, so he decided to let it go for now.

While in the car, Coleman took a call, and Sean was sure he was the subject of it. It intensified his discomfort. "Let's go shopping," Coleman announced with a smirk. Sean didn't comment but waited for an explanation. "The person I have working on your place sent me a list of things that she needs."

"Needs for what?" Sean questioned.

"Needs for your place," Coleman answered.

"I don't need anything," Sean stated emphatically.

Coleman cast a sideways glance at him and smiled. "Apparently, you do." He understood Sean's reluctance to accept help, but he wanted him to have a decent home. After seeing the apartment Sean had been living in for six weeks, he was so riddled with guilt that it was going to take a lot of gifts and help before he felt even a little better. "The furnishings from your last place, was any of it important to you? Any family heirlooms among them?"

"No, it's just stuff I got at the thrift shop on Fourth Street."

"Good, then you won't mind if those items are returned to the thrift shop, and I get you new furniture. That old stuff just didn't look good in your new place."

"I'm fine. Really. I am only going to be here another six weeks, and I don't need much." Sean attempted to dissuade Coleman from buying him things.

"Just a few things, Sean. A chair, sofa, table, bed…just a few things." It was obvious Coleman was not going to be thwarted.

Sean was floored when they pulled into an Ethan Allen showroom. "Ethan Allen? Really? Can't we just do… House of Bargains?" His sarcasm elicited immediate laughter from Coleman.

"I'm the one shopping, and I don't shop House of Bargains. They never have anything I like." Coleman continued laughing. He wasn't being condescending; it was just a pure statement of preference.

Coleman quickly went about checking and evaluating various pieces of furniture. The salesman stuck close to him, knowing a large sale was at hand. Sean managed to slip to the side and wandered about on his own. He was not a shopper and did not enjoy picking out furniture. It surprised him that Coleman took such an interest in putting together the right look for him. He didn't realize that Coleman would enjoy interior decorating, or that he had such a good eye for color and balance in a space. It was out of character for him, or so it seemed to Sean.

"There you are," Coleman said as he walked toward Sean, who was aimlessly browsing the overstuffed pillow section. He brought him around and showed him the items he had selected and told him they would be delivered and set up today.

Sean could not believe the cost—it was in the thousands. Everything was amazing in its beauty, structure, elegance; it was all breathtaking. "Is this all due to guilt?" Sean finally asked when they were leaving.

"Yes, pretty much all guilt," Coleman admitted. His honesty caught Sean off guard and he started to laugh out loud. It was heartfelt, deep, genuine laughter. Coleman playfully put his arm around Sean's neck and pulled him to him, kissing him on the cheek and then hugging him to his chest. Sean just continued to laugh. Coleman took out his phone and asked to snap a quick picture of the two of them. Sean agreed and leaned in for the photo. They walked together like that to Coleman's car and were still laughing when they drove away.

"I have an appointment at four," Coleman said as he reached into the storage compartment between the seats and pulled out a computer tablet. "Will you act as my assistant and take notes?"

Sean wondered if it was going to be another ruse, like last night, but it turned out to be a genuine client. It was a corporate issue and the meeting was at the client's home in a secluded suburb where many wealthy businessmen and their families resided. Sean was concerned that his casual dress would not be appropriate but Coleman didn't seem bothered by it, and as it turned out the meeting took place in the client's greenhouse. He was an avid gardener and spent every weekend working with his beloved plants. The experience was one Sean never thought he'd get. He was able to watch Coleman in action discussing, evaluating, and manipulating a case. It wasn't a big or important case, but still, given the level of detail, Sean could have been forgiven for thinking it was his only case. *This is how he became who he is*, Sean thought. *He gives every case the impression of being his only case. Every client is his most important client.*

Once back in the car, Sean attempted to return the computer tablet to him, but Coleman told him to keep it. "Send the notes to my address—it is in the computer—and keep the pad; it will be useful for you." Sean put the pad into his messenger bag and did not comment. "Here, take this too." Coleman handed him a state-of-the-art cell phone. "It contains my entire Rolodex and you may add any of your personal numbers that you wish."

"Thank you, sir."

"Outside of the office, you are welcome to call me Coleman."

Sean considered this for some time before deciding that he would never call him Coleman outside of his own head. He could think of him as Coleman, but never verbalize it. He would be "sir" or "Mr. West." The familiarity of a first name did not feel right to him. Sean was just an intern, not a friend. Coleman was simply being kind and that would eventually wear off and he, low-class, ill-bred Sean Robbins, did not want to be caught calling him "Coleman" when it did. He did not say any of this, but instead nodded and let it go.

Despite himself, Sean was anxiously looking forward to seeing his apartment. He knew the furniture Coleman had chosen would look perfect in the apartment and wanted to see how the decorator set it up. He was torn with regard to the gifts. Part of him saw it as a strange way of making up for rejecting his application, while the other part saw it as a kindness. He decided to go with the kindness and just enjoy the things while he was there.

"So what do you think?" Coleman handed him the keys as they entered the apartment and started walking around.

"This is more than I ever expected." Sean walked around, running his hand along the smooth wood of the dining-room table and then across the lush leather of the sofa and recliner. The room smelled of quality wood and leather. It smelled rich. The kitchen was stocked with the essential appliances and a set of china. The bedroom was just as impressive. The bed was large and soft, and everything matched. The bed matched the table and dressers, and the comforter matched the rugs and window treatments. "The person you hired to put this all together did a very good job." Sean smiled a smile of appreciation.

"She is a professional. I hired her to do my own apartment and my estate." Coleman felt good having provided for Sean and seeing the smile on his face. He looked at the bed and was instantly flooded with an urge that he fought to suppress. His relationship with Sean was not at that level, and he needed to take it slow. Finally, he left the room in order to push the urge into the background and regain control. "I am going to leave you now and let you get comfortable in your new home. Enjoy. See you Monday."

He quickly vacated the apartment, leaving Sean wondering what he'd done wrong.

Once in the hallway, Coleman took a deep breath and tried to calm his heartbeat. He had not felt desire so strong and sudden since… he couldn't remember a time. That thought elicited a painful laugh as he got into the elevator and willed himself down to the car. He desperately wanted to go back to Sean and beg him to let him stay the night. Their relationship at present was intern and supervisor, which did not leave room for romantic involvement. Having Sean as an intern at his firm definitely had its positives and negatives. Coleman would have him around him on a daily basis, but he could not establish a relationship with him until the internship ended. This was going to be a pain-filled six weeks, he realized. He remembered their first kiss last night. Sean had not resisted and had not made an issue of it. And also there was the kiss this afternoon; Sean had enjoyed and accepted his kiss. This thought brought hope to Coleman that he would be able to get through the next six weeks as long as he could look forward to a kiss from time to time.

FIVE

SEAN watched Coleman leave. It was an awkward exit. He wanted to be away from him—Sean felt it. He instantly started reliving the past few minutes, trying to discover what he'd done that had made Coleman uncomfortable and necessitated his departure. He couldn't think of anything in particular that could have caused it. But he knew he had to be much more careful in his words and his actions. He would maintain professionalism and respect and he would work hard at his internship. Sean pulled out the cell-phone that Coleman had provided him and dialed Mr. Murray's number.

"Hello, Mr. Murray." Sean had promised to call him and report the evening's outcome. Ed was a good man and he seemed genuinely concerned about him.

"Are you okay?" Murray asked. "What happened with West?"

"It was a strange night and an even stranger day," Sean began, and as he continued to talk to Ed, he went to the kitchen and brewed himself a cup of coffee. "He drove me home but wouldn't let me stay there. He said it was too dangerous."

Ed broke in and questioned him about his residence. Like Coleman, he became unglued. He'd had no idea that Sean had been residing in such an area. He tore into him and lectured him on the importance of being careful and checking out an area before moving in. "Do you have any idea how many murders occurred this year in that end of town?"

"No."

"Well, I do, and so does Mr. West. There is nothing strange about him not allowing you to stay there; it is a matter of common sense."

"I spent the night at his estate in the country." Sean went right in for the shock value. "There was nothing to it," he explained quickly, in case Ed got the wrong idea. "I slept in his guest room. He made me breakfast in the morning and took me to town and set me up in an apartment. He also paid to have the place furnished. He hired a decorator to do it." He took a long sip of the coffee he'd just poured as he let it all sink in for Ed.

Ed didn't know what to say. He had no knowledge of an estate in the country. Coleman was always contacted, if he had to be contacted, at the apartment in the city. It was a large, expensive apartment that everyone assumed was his home. The information about a country home was strangely comforting. The man was more than just a suit and a job. But why would he take Sean to his country home? The comfort he'd briefly experienced evaporated. Coleman was not kind, and he was not considerate when it came to individuals who broke his rules. Sean had gone around him and acquired a placement in spite of his disapproval. He would view this as a deliberate assault on his leadership. He'd have to make an example of Sean in some way to show others not to attempt the same.

"I'm standing in the apartment right now. It is beautiful. He also took me to lunch and had me take notes for him at a business meeting he had with a client. I don't know what to make of it. What do you think?" Sean decided not to mention the two times he'd kissed him. The one this afternoon was minor, just a friendly peck on the cheek, but the one last night had been different. There had been no threat or intimidation in it, but there was a depth to it, a definite sensuality Sean admitted he had not resisted.

"I don't know what to think, Sean," Ed began. "Everything he is doing with you and the way he is treating you is unlike the man that I have worked for the past five years. All I can say, and I can't stress it enough, is be careful, son. Be careful, and if you need a place to stay, you are welcome to move in with me and my wife. Our kids are all away at college and there is plenty of room. Don't stay in that apartment if you feel the least bit uncomfortable or threatened."

"I think it is okay. I really don't believe he means me any harm. I asked him why he was doing all of this. I asked him if it was because of guilt, and he said yes. He feels guilty for rejecting my application and for me living in that fleabag apartment, as he called it." Sean was trying to convince himself as much as he was trying to convince Ed. Did Coleman mean him any harm? Who knew? Only time would tell, but he wanted to ease any worries Ed might have had. His concern was becoming evident in the tone of his voice, and Sean didn't want to saddle Ed with any of his fears.

"I hope you're right, but my offer still stands."

"Yes, sir."

COLEMAN did not return to the estate. Instead he went to his apartment in the city. He wanted to be closer to Sean. Sean's apartment was less than two blocks from his, and he could easily walk there if need be. He wasn't sure why he felt the need to be nearby this weekend, but he did. It probably had something to do with the overwhelming sexual desire he'd felt while in Sean's apartment. He laughed at the thought. He had a reputation for loose and shallow relationships, and it was a reputation he'd come by honestly. He preferred acquaintances, not relationships. He couldn't abide hangers-on—the people who wouldn't go away or demanded your time and your interest long after your desire for involvement had vanished. He thought about Sean and wondered if he would be a hanger-on. Would he know enough to go away when their time was over? That thought made him stop in his tracks and catch his breath as if he'd just been slapped. The thought of Sean going away filled him with an uneasiness that was baffling. The more he considered the thought, the more anxious he became, until finally, he grabbed his cell phone and called Sean. He needed to confirm for himself that Sean was still there.

"How's the apartment? Do you have everything you need?" He relaxed immediately upon hearing Sean's voice. This was the most irrational thing he had ever done in his life, but he had to do it.

"The place is very nice, and thanks. I didn't have time to thank you before… before you left." Sean was surprised to hear from him but also pleased, strangely enough. Coleman was the last person on earth he ever thought he would want to hear from, but here he was, all excited about a phone call. "I wanted to thank you for the groceries, also. It wasn't necessary, but I appreciate it."

"You're welcome." Coleman fell silent for a few moments. "Sean, last night you told me that you don't hate me; you don't like me, but you don't hate me either. What can I do to make you like me?"

Sean was taken aback by this statement. He laughed nervously before answering. "You care if I like you?"

"Yes."

"Why?"

"I value your opinion."

"Again, why?"

Coleman wanted to tell him he was enraptured and spending time with him was a pure delight, but he couldn't tell him that, not yet anyway. He wanted Sean to like him, he *needed* him to like him, and he craved his approval. "I'd like for us to be friends, if that is possible," Coleman said finally.

"I won't lie to you; it's hard to like you because I don't trust you. But I will say that I like you more today than I did yesterday. As far as being friends, you might want to rethink that request considering my limited social structure. I doubt having me as a friend would be good for your reputation." Sean was surprised he was able to voice so many of his feelings without faltering.

"So, you memorized the letter," Coleman said and started to laugh. "Your social structure will not be an issue for me. Besides, I know that having you as a friend could only be an improvement for me. I look forward to tomorrow, and the next day, when you will like me even more than you do today." He laughed and Sean joined him. He changed the subject. "What are you doing?"

"Drinking a cup of coffee."

"There is a casual restaurant on the bottom floor of the building next to yours—meet me there in thirty minutes." Coleman then hung up. He didn't wait for a yes or a no; he expected him to be there in thirty minutes.

Sean hurried to grab his jacket and lock up the apartment. He wasn't sure where the restaurant was and wanted to be there when Coleman arrived. When he walked in, the head waiter asked his name, and apparently, Coleman had already called and reserved a table for them. He was led to a secluded table at the back of the restaurant. Coleman had said it was a casual restaurant, but it appeared high-end to Sean. He wished he was dressed a little better. He ordered a cup of coffee and waited.

Coleman could not explain why he wanted to meet Sean. The restaurant was an excuse to get together. He had hung up for fear that Sean would have other plans or not want to meet him. He didn't know what he was going say to him. All Coleman knew was he needed to see him. He had never felt like this in his life. Never had he been so compelled to be near someone. He needed to figure this out, he told himself, and in the meantime, he wanted to speak with Sean. As soon as he entered, he knew Sean was there; he felt him in the room. The waiter led him to the secluded table. Sean stood up and put out his hand as soon as Coleman approached the table.

Coleman took his hand, but then smiled and said, "I think we're beyond the handshake, don't you?" and pulled Sean to him and kissed him full on the lips. It was a hungry, tender, exploring kiss that probably lasted longer than it should have. He'd been thinking about his next kiss ever since he had left Sean's apartment and couldn't resist taking the opportunity when it presented itself. He quickly changed the subject before Sean had too much time to think about it. "More coffee? How about a drink?" He noticed what Sean was drinking and suggested something a little stronger.

Sean leaned slightly away from him and looked in his eyes. He was checking for motive and intent, but all he saw was acceptance. Coleman's behavior and attitude was beginning to startle him. He had written the most biased, hateful rejection letter Sean had ever seen, and yet here he was, treating him like he was important—valued, even. It was becoming difficult to understand. Coleman ordered a scotch for himself and asked Sean what he wanted to drink. Sean was not a drinker, so he asked for the same.

They talked about a variety of subjects, including Sean's internship assignment. Coleman wanted him to transfer from Ed and become his intern.

"You have an intern: Brittany Saunders," Sean stated.

"Miss Saunders is working with my assistant, Janet Hendricks. I never actually take an intern on myself," Coleman clarified.

"So the sought-after, prestigious position with Mr. Coleman West is actually just a ruse." Sean smiled and took a deep swallow of the scotch.

"Yes, just a facade. Sorry." Coleman laughed, finished his drink, and ordered two more for them. "I would like to work with you. I would like for you to be my intern... my real intern," he proposed.

"I like working with Mr. Murray. I would prefer to stay with him." The second scotch made Sean feel much more relaxed "He took a big risk with me, and I owe him my loyalty. I will not leave him willingly."

"I thought you'd say that, but I wanted to make the offer anyway. Ed would understand, you know." Coleman took another drink and so did Sean. "He would want you to get the best experience possible during your placement." Coleman ordered them both another drink.

"I couldn't imagine a better experience than the one I am having with Mr. Murray."

"Ouch!" Coleman said and laughed. "Oh, such a wounding remark." He pretended to be hurt by what Sean had said.

Sean withdrew slightly, not sure if he was serious or joking. He took another long sip of his drink and Coleman ordered them both another. He was beginning to feel the alcohol, so slowed down on the second drink.

Coleman recognized Sean was experiencing intoxication by the slight slurring of his words and a subtle loss of coordination. He realized then that Sean was probably not accustomed to strong drink and it had hit him hard and fast. Coleman had not intended for this to happen but saw it as an opportunity to ask some questions and to get some honest answers.

"Is being a legal assistant your life's dream?" Coleman began to explore. He sensed more to Sean than a legal assistant. He was good at his job, no question about that, but there was more to him than this.

"No," Sean answered immediately, without thought. "I was an art student before my mother became ill. After her death, I just wanted to get a degree fast that would provide a decent wage and allow me to get a job quickly." Sean swayed in his seat, trying desperately to bring Coleman's face into proper focus. "I needed to get on with life and stop screwing around with pipe dreams."

"Are you an artist?"

"Depends on who you ask." He smiled. "My mother thought I was a genius, and my professor thought I was... okay." He rubbed his face, trying to clear the imaginary cobwebs he felt there. "But then he was a purist, and I was a realist. Not a happy couple." Sean finished the scotch, but Coleman did not order another.

Coleman reached out and steadied him by holding onto his upper arm.

"The room is spinning. I need to go home." Sean made to get up but didn't succeed. Before he hit the floor, Coleman grabbed him, hauled him up to lean against his side, and held him there, supporting his entire weight with one arm as he motioned for the waiter to come over.

"Yes, sir, can I help you?" The waiter tried to assist him with Sean, but Coleman waved him off.

"I've got him," he said and then asked the waiter to call them a cab. "I'm going to take him outside for some fresh air."

Sean was vaguely aware of what was happening but had no ability to respond. Coleman helped him outside the restaurant, holding him up with one arm around his waist. Sean, in his alcohol-fueled haze, was impressed by his strength. His feet were barely touching the ground. Coleman was supporting his entire weight with just one arm. "Thank you," Sean mumbled.

"You're welcome." Coleman reached over with his free hand and brushed the hair back from Sean's face. "I'm going to take you home with me tonight."

"Okay," Sean answered, his ability to question and reason completely gone.

Coleman eased him into the cab and then followed him in, propping him up against him. Sean completely passed out and gradually slid down and ended up with his head in Coleman's lap. Coleman didn't move him but let him rest there until they reached their destination. Both the cab driver and the doorman offered to help him with Sean, but again he declined assistance. "Wake up, Sean." Coleman prodded him to a standing position, and with an arm around him, began walking him toward the elevators. Sean groaned and his head rolled from side to side, landing on Coleman's shoulder, where, once again, he passed out. Coleman supported his entire weight and held him tight against him while the elevator took them to the top floor.

Sean forced one eye open and looked up at Coleman. "I'm sorry." The words were scarcely audible as his face was pressed against Coleman's chest.

"Think nothing of it." Coleman was laughing when he planted a tender kiss on Sean's forehead. Upon exiting the elevator, Coleman picked Sean up and threw him over his shoulder, carrying him fireman-style. Once inside his apartment, he took Sean to the guest room and deposited him on the bed. Coleman removed Sean's jacket and then his shirt. Sean was like a rag doll lying on the bed. Coleman took his shoes and socks off first, and then, with a heavy sigh, undid Sean's jeans and slid them down and off. Sean lay there before him in only a T-shirt and briefs. Coleman took in every aspect of his body, which was slender, yet solid and muscular. He was an extremely attractive man, and Coleman stood there for some time, appreciating the vision before him. He picked Sean up in order to pull the comforter back and then placed him under the covers. Sean threw his arms around his neck in an awkward attempt to steady himself.

"I love you, man." Sean slurred, never opening his eyes.

Coleman smiled and tucked the blankets around him. He bent down and again kissed his forehead. "I love you too, man."

Coleman left the room, went to his own room, and dressed for bed in a pair of soft pajama pants. Just as he was settling down, he heard a loud thump from the guest bedroom. Instantly he leaped out of bed and ran into Sean's room. Sean was on the floor, either fast asleep or unconscious. Coleman bent down and scooped him up, then laid him back down and again tucked him in.

"Good night," he whispered, and Sean moaned. After Sean rolled out of bed and hit the floor for the second time, Coleman decided it would be better if he took him to his room. He wasn't sure how Sean would feel about it in the morning, but it had to be done. Coleman needed to sleep, and Sean needed to stop hitting the floor.

Coleman carried him to his room, laid him in the center of the bed, and then slid in next to him. He pulled the blankets up to cover them both and put his arm around Sean, then pulled him to him in a tight hug in a spooning position. Sean wouldn't be able to roll off now without taking Coleman with him. Sean snuggled in and threaded his fingers through Coleman's, holding him tightly. Coleman pressed his face into the crook of Sean's neck, inhaling the fresh scent of his hair and skin. "Oh," he groaned, "this could prove troublesome." Sean stirred in his sleep and bent his head to place a kiss on the back of Coleman's hand, which was near his face.

"I love you, man," he moaned.

Coleman was touched by the gentleness of the gesture. He kissed Sean's ear and feathered kisses down his neck and across his shoulder. "Good night, Sean." He wondered if Sean even knew who he was with.

"Good night, Coleman," Sean answered. Coleman squeezed him even tighter and buried his face against his shoulder.

SEAN came awake slowly. His eyes felt like they had been glued shut. As the room came into focus, so did the muscular arm draped possessively across his upper body. Realization hit him that he was being held tightly against someone. Sean was not in bed alone. He turned his head and came face-to-face with the sleeping person sharing his pillow and holding him tightly. His heart leaped into his throat as sheer panic engulfed him. *What did I do? What happened?* Sean glanced around the room, but nothing looked familiar. He reasoned that he must be in Coleman's apartment in the city, but why were they in bed together? Sean struggled to remember, but there was nothing after the second scotch at the restaurant. The rest of the evening was a blur.

Coleman felt Sean's heart begin to race. He responded by pulling him closer, into a tender embrace. "You're okay. Nothing happened. We just slept in the same bed," he said softly into Sean's ear. His hot breath fanned the side of Sean's face, and Coleman could feel Sean's breathing and his loss of control.

This can't be happening to me. Sean scrambled to focus on anything other than the feel, the smell, the presence, of the man lying next to him. "I'm sorry," Sean managed to squeeze out between labored breaths.

"Don't be. It was as much my fault as yours. I shouldn't have bought you all those drinks." Coleman yawned and gathered Sean even closer. Then he snuggled back down and closed his eyes. He wasn't ready to get up yet, and he wasn't ready to let Sean get up. "It's early—go back to sleep."

Sean was on high alert. Every inch of him that was pressed against Coleman was warm and tingling. He made note of his hard stomach, hips, and firm thighs, all molded to him and hot, smoldering hot. *Stop thinking!* he chastised himself and forced himself to try to remember the previous night. How had he ended up here? *Relax, just relax. He said nothing happened and he doesn't sound angry.* Sean continued to coach himself in order to calm his heart and his breathing. After about fifteen to twenty minutes of Sean desperately trying to relax and not succeeding, he spoke to Coleman.

"What did I do last night? Did I embarrass myself or you?" His voice was so sad, so pained that Coleman pulled himself up onto his elbow in order to look down into Sean's anguished face.

"You didn't do anything. You just passed out at the restaurant," Coleman told him gently.

"How did I get here?"

"I carried you. You're not very large, so it wasn't difficult."

"I'm sorry."

"Stop with the sorry, I don't want to hear it anymore." Coleman gave him the dark stare that told him he'd had enough. "I have you in bed with me because you kept falling out of the bed in the guest room." Coleman figured he might as well explain that point as well because he knew it was going to come up.

"Did I say anything offensive?"

Coleman thought for a moment before responding. "You kept telling me you were sorry, and twice you told me that you loved me."

"I say that to everyone when I've had too much to drink." Sean tried to explain away any awkwardness that might arise from his declaration.

"I thought as much, but I enjoyed it anyway, and will treasure the memory." Coleman started to laugh and collapsed on top of Sean, who was slowly calming and seeing the situation for what it was. Without thinking, he threw his arms around Coleman and hugged him. Coleman gave a deep sigh followed by a groan. "I had better let you up now, or I may never let you go." He kissed him quickly and then rolled off to stand by the side of the bed, leaving Sean still on his back in the middle of the bed. Sean suddenly started laughing uncontrollably and rolled onto his side. His entire body shook with laughter. "Hey! What's so funny?" Coleman faked offense while looking down at himself standing there in his thin pajama pants.

"I have to call Professor Weir and give him my weekly progress report today." Sean had a hard time talking through his laughter. "I think I will leave this part out." He sat up, still laughing. "I attended court, a dinner party, an individual client interview, and then I got drunk and slept with Coleman West. I don't think he would be impressed."

Coleman smiled broadly. "He might not be impressed, but I certainly am." He winked at him and said, "Pull it together, and I will take you to breakfast."

Sean made to get up and the effects of last night hit him. His head started to throb and his stomach began to churn. "Oh, I don't think I can do breakfast. My head is suddenly killing me, and I think I'm going to...." He jumped off the bed and ran but didn't know where the bathroom was. Sensing what he needed, Coleman grabbed his hand and pulled him to the master bath as quickly as he could.

Sean knelt in front of the toilet and began to heave and heave. He started shaking again but not with laughter. Coleman crouched down beside him and began rubbing his shoulders and his back as Sean continued to heave. Sean couldn't believe Coleman was being so kind and caring. He was rubbing his back, and the fact that Sean was vomiting uncontrollably in his bathroom didn't seem to bother him. Sean leaned both arms on the toilet seat as he hung his head over the bowl. He cocked his head to one side and was about to speak to Coleman.

"I know, you're sorry." Coleman laughed. He took a wet washcloth and wiped Sean's face and then helped him to a standing position. "Under control?" he asked. He was referring to the vomiting.

"I think so."

Coleman gave him a toothbrush and toothpaste and waited while he freshened his mouth. "I think you better go back to bed for now." He helped Sean back to the bed and tucked him in.

"I love you, man," Sean teased.

"I love you too, Sean," Coleman shot back. He let him rest for a couple of hours and then brought him aspirin and something to drink. By two in the afternoon, Sean was dressed and said he was well enough to walk home if Coleman would tell him how to get there. Coleman persuaded Sean to sit for a few minutes and have another cup of coffee.

"Last night, you told me that you were originally an art student and had aspirations of making a career in fine art."

"Wow, I did a lot of talking," Sean diverted.

"Tell me about it," Coleman persisted.

"Yes, I did have that dream at one time, but then reality punched me in the face and I decided to get a real career." Sean downplayed his talent.

"How far had you gotten before you quit?" Coleman was not going to let the subject go.

"I finished. I have a degree in fine art, for whatever that is worth. I went back to school before mom got sick to get my Legal Studies degree, so as to actually make a living." He noticed Coleman raise his eyebrows in surprise.

"Have I seen any of your work?"

"Not unless you've been in my bedroom," Sean stated sarcastically, and then he continued, "I haven't had any noteworthy commissions."

"I want to see some of your work," Coleman said and then went to get his coat. "Do you have any at your apartment?"

"A few pieces, not much." Sean was confused.

Coleman threw Sean his coat and said, "Come on, let's go."

"Where?"

"I'm walking you home and you are going to show me your work." Coleman locked the door and they walked together to the elevator.

"How close is my apartment?" Sean thought it must be fairly close if they were going to walk there. His next thought was *Why did Coleman get me an apartment so close to his?* Probably just a coincidence, he decided.

"Two blocks north." Coleman watched Sean lean against the elevator wall and stare at the floor. This morning's intimacy was fading, and Sean's fear and distrust were returning. He really didn't like people to know too much about him. It was something Coleman could relate to. Sean looked decidedly uncomfortable, but Coleman needed to know the level of his talent, needed to know if he could have a career in art. He wanted to help him to aspire to his dream and not to just settle. "It's okay, Sean."

"What if you hate them?" Sean voiced his fear.

"Then you will go back to school and take more art courses. If this is what you want to do as a career, and last night you said that it was, then you shouldn't let anything get in your way. I believe your work is probably very good and all you lack is confidence." They left the building and headed north in silence. Coleman reached over and took Sean's hand, holding it loosely in his as they walked.

When they got to Sean's apartment, Sean brought out the few sketches of the city that he had completed during his off time. Coleman was impressed. Sean had more talent than he had even expected. Sean then showed him some graphic work he had completed. One piece was of special interest to him. It depicted a man, a building, and paper, paper everywhere of every type—newspaper, legal paper, wrapping paper. The color use was severe as was the man.

"Is this me?" Coleman eyed him closely as he answered.

"Maybe," Sean said softly.

"Is this how you see me?"

"Maybe," Sean repeated. "I completed it before I knew you."

"I'm glad to hear that."

They talked about school in general, and then Coleman discussed possible art schools in the area where Sean could continue his training. He also asked to see samples of his commission work. He hadn't missed the statement earlier that Sean had completed some commissioned pieces. Sean hedged around actually committing to letting him see more of his work.

"All of this interest in my art career is a little unsettling," Sean commented as he took the sketches and returned them to his room. "Are you trying to tell me something about my ability as a legal assistant?"

"Definitely not. Ed tells me you're a first-rate assistant, but I believe a person should do what they enjoy. Work for satisfaction, not just a paycheck."

Coleman decided to let it go for now. He would consider the options available for Sean and present them at a later time. Sean's work was so good he could be a professional artist.

Sean appreciated his opinion and his positive remarks. It gave him something to think about. He had about six more weeks before his internship would be finished, and he would graduate shortly after. With a legal-assistant certification in hand, would it be wise to pursue a career in art? He would have to think about it. Sean hadn't shown Coleman all of the work he had at the apartment. Several pieces meant a lot to him, and he wasn't ready for others to see them. Besides, Coleman couldn't possibly be interested in his future.

"Are you satisfied with being a lawyer? Do you enjoy what you are doing?" Sean threw it out there and waited to see if Coleman would answer.

Coleman considered the question for a time before responding, and when he did he held Sean's gaze and took a step closer to him, as if he were telling him something of great importance and he needed Sean to hear him clearly. "I am a lawyer, and I am a stonemason." Coleman waited for his reaction.

"A stonemason?" Sean smiled and remembered all the detailed stone work at Coleman's estate. "You did all of the work at your estate yourself?" Sean recalled the porch, the patio, and the inlay floors and was amazed again. Coleman nodded. "Your work is great."

"Thank you, and to answer your question, yes, I enjoy being a lawyer as much as I enjoy working with stone." Few people knew of his hobby; he rarely shared this part of himself with others. But he wanted to get closer to Sean and to do so, he had to open up.

They spent the next few hours discussing personal interests with regard to food, movies, books, television, politics, music, and every other question Coleman could possibly edge into the conversation. He made it seem casual, but he was taking note of everything Sean said. Sean leaned heavily Democratic whereas he was more of a fiscal Republican, which Coleman saw as an opportunity for spirited conversations. In every other area, they seemed to concur with just slight variations in taste and preference. Coleman pondered the thought that although they had been born into very different lives and circumstances, they were very similar people. Similar except for Sean's hint of naiveté, an aspect of his personality that Coleman had never possessed. Coleman had been cold and analytical since the day he was born, yet he found this trait in Sean very endearing.

Sean made him dinner, which Coleman enjoyed immensely. Sean prepared pork chops with baked potatoes and a green salad. For dessert, he served baked apples with ice cream, one of Sean's favorites.

Coleman was impressed and asked him where he'd learned how to cook.

"My mother always worked at least two jobs, so I usually had the job of preparing the meals. I learned everything I know from the *Betty Crocker Cookbook*. I discovered that if you can read, you can cook." Sean smiled and offered Coleman a cup of coffee to go with his dessert.

"Thank you, yes," Coleman said and then added, "Not everyone who reads can cook. It takes talent and an understanding of how foods go together." He finished his dessert and said, "You're an excellent cook."

"Thank you, and with praise like that, you are welcome back here for dinner any day." Sean was touched by the compliment. It meant a lot coming from someone like Coleman, a man who'd probably had the best there was as far as meals went.

Coleman stayed until about nine o'clock. He helped Sean clean up after dinner, and then they sat in the living room and talked more about Sean's art career. Coleman suggested that he put together a portfolio of his work and start shopping it around.

Sean was unsure about putting himself out there to that degree. Shopping himself around would take some real nerve, and he didn't believe he possessed that level of confidence yet. He felt he had to be better before he could take the risk of self-promotion. He didn't say any of this to Coleman because he wouldn't understand. Coleman was a man who always got what he wanted. He never let lack of nerve or the opinions of others stand in his way. He wouldn't grasp Sean's fear of rejection; it was something Coleman probably had little, if any, experience with.

"Think about it," Coleman urged as he got his coat from the closet and prepared to leave. He found himself not in a hurry. He moved toward Sean and reached out to glide his hand along his cheek and slip in behind his neck, gently pulling Sean to him. Sean's gaze held him in an almost hypnotic trance as he lowered his head to take Sean's lips in a tender kiss. He placed his other hand on the small of Sean's back and pressed him firmly against him. Gradually, he teased Sean's lips apart and then entered to taste and seductively explore.

Sean embraced him lightly with a hand on either side of his waist. He was losing himself in the experience and sensation that was Coleman. His tongue was doing things that set loose sensations through Sean's groin. Sean groaned and tightened his embrace, fully immersed in the feeling of Coleman's hands and his mouth. Sean felt Coleman's hot breath in his mouth and trembled with instant, nearly overwhelming desire.

Coleman slowed and carefully stroked his lips and then trailed sensual caresses down to Sean's throat, where he inhaled deeply and stated breathlessly, "I'd better go."

Sean agreed with a nod. Words were beyond him at the moment. He released Coleman as soon as his mind registered the statement, "I'd better go," and he attempted to back off.

Coleman's release was much slower in coming. He loosened his grip but did not immediately let go. Instead he let his hands travel the expanse of Sean's back several times and then dropped his hands and took hold of both of Sean's hands. "You're a good companion, Sean. I enjoyed our time together yesterday, last night, and today." He smiled broadly, remembering Sean last night and the events of this morning.

Sean followed the direction of his thoughts and immediately said, "I'm sorry for my behavior last night. I'm sorry for being a burden to you."

Coleman's smile instantly dropped, and he stated very clearly, "You're no burden. I had a good time, and it all helped me to get to know you better. If you hadn't gotten drunk, I probably wouldn't have learned about your art degree for months, or discovered that you fall in love very easily when intoxicated." He gave him a quick kiss on the lips and then turned to go. "May I call you?"

"Sure, if you want to." Sean wasn't sure what "call you" meant, but it sounded harmless.

"I want to." The smile returned as Coleman's gaze traveled Sean's face, taking in every aspect of it. He left, closing the door softly behind him.

SIX

SEAN settled into his apartment, put on his pajamas and slippers after Coleman left, and then called the professor to give him a summary of his experiences this week. In the past weeks he'd had the usual court, depositions, and paperwork, but this week he had attended a dinner party, observed Coleman interviewing a client, and got to hang out with Coleman for most of the weekend. He thought the professor would be quite impressed with his accomplishments. But again, he was not going to mention the drunkenness or waking up in bed with Coleman.

There just wasn't any way of explaining it without it sounding whorish. He smiled to himself. *Coleman would not be wasting his time with someone like me. Like the receptionist said, he is with someone new every week and they are always the cream of society.* Sean laughed; he'd never been described as the cream of society—the debris of society, yes, but never the cream. He didn't have a chance in hell of ever being considered by Coleman as anything other than a lowly intern.

Although, for the moment, Coleman's guilt was affording him a few extra perks.

THE following week went by rather quickly. Ed had several cases to present and Sean was made a part of his legal team. He told him, "You might as well get a feel for it, Sean, it is going to be your career," so he let Sean accompany him on client visits and court hearings and backroom dealings. Sean was impressed with Ed's mediation skills. He could bring the most hateful, argumentative, emotionally distant people together and make them see and accept each other's views. It was an education Sean felt was of great value and that he would use.

As of Thursday, Coleman had not called, and Sean was beginning to think that perhaps the guilt had worn off and he would no longer be attended to. It was a sad feeling, and he felt a little abandoned. He knew it was stupid to be feeling anything other than regret about his dealings with Coleman. But a part of him yearned to feel his touch and to smell the fresh, laundered aroma of his clothing and intense manliness. He stopped himself immediately and forced himself to calm down. Thoughts of the several embraces and kisses and the time spent with Coleman were pleasurable, but not healthy or productive. "Life goes on, Sean," he said to himself sternly, "and you are not part of his crowd. Remember, no one except the best of society, and even they only get a week." Sean laughed out loud and had turned from his desk to go return several resource manuals when he was caught by two hands, one on each shoulder. He found himself halted in his tracks and stared up into the face of the man he'd so recently been daydreaming about. He fought the rising crimson in his face and tried to look unaffected.

"Slow down, you nearly ran me over," Coleman stated good-naturedly.

"Sorry, I didn't see you," Sean apologized quickly.

Coleman let his hands remain where they were for a few moments. "Where are you going in such a hurry?"

"Just the library. I wanted to return these volumes before five." Sean backed up then, as if expecting Coleman to step aside and let him pass. But he stayed put, completely blocking the exit from the back office. Sean stood silent and waited.

"I called you last night," Coleman stated suddenly. "I called you three times. Is there a reason you're not taking my calls?" He stood there, filling the room and demanding an explanation while speaking in a calm and soothing tone.

"I went for a walk," Sean began to clarify very quickly. "I didn't take the phone with me. I'm sorry, I haven't checked it either. I didn't realize anyone had called. I'm not that attached to cell phones because it was an extra bill that I could do without." His explanation went on like this for a few more minutes before Coleman raised his hand in a bid for him to stop.

"What about your professor? Weren't you concerned he might try to call you?" Coleman did not like taking a backseat to Weir.

"I don't sit and wait anxiously for him to call me," Sean said with an edge to his voice. "I'm not that whipped. Besides, he doesn't call students, they call him."

"I'm glad to hear that, but I would appreciate it if you would start to carry your phone and answer it once in a while." Coleman, too, had a bit of an edge.

"Yes, sir, I will, and I'm sorry." Sean was sincere. He wished he'd gotten Coleman's call. He had been hoping to hear from him, but hadn't really believed he would call. It bothered Sean that he'd missed his calls.

"Do you have it with you now?" Coleman smiled and reached out to run his fingers along Sean's jaw in an intimate gesture that surprised Sean, considering they were at work.

"No. I left it at the apartment. I'm not used to carrying one, and I forget."

"We are going to have to pull you into the twenty-first century, Sean." Coleman stared at him with a devouring kind of look and then turned away toward the door. "Are you busy tonight?"

"No," Sean said abruptly.

"I'll pick you up at seven," Coleman said and then left without adding further detail.

Sean was excited about the date but concerned that perhaps he'd offended Coleman by not getting his call. He kicked himself for not thinking to keep that blasted phone with him. Of course he would call him on the cell. What had he been thinking, sitting around waiting for a call and then leaving for a walk around town and not taking the stupid thing with him? Sean beat himself up for the better part of an hour.

Coleman left feeling better than he had since yesterday evening when Sean failed to answer his third call. He had thought perhaps Sean had been upset because he hadn't called him sooner, but that didn't seem like him. Sean wasn't that needy or expectant, but Coleman was worried that he'd ruined things by waiting. He didn't want to come on too strong, considering he'd monopolized Sean's entire weekend, and he'd thought it best to give Sean some time to process and hopefully look forward to seeing him. But having his calls ignored had been... upsetting. It was a great relief to discover Sean was simply technologically backward and not angry. He smiled at the thought of someone in this day and age not being comfortable carrying a cell phone. Sean was definitely a special twenty-three-year-old; not using to a cell phone was a true anomaly for a young man.

Sean hurried to get everything Ed had requested accomplished by five o'clock. Usually, he would work overtime getting everything prepared when Ed had a hearing in the morning, but tonight he wanted to get home early enough to clean the apartment and get himself ready. Coleman hadn't told him where they were going or what they were going to do, so he assumed it wasn't something he had to dress up for. Sean chose his best jeans, a dark- blue button-down cotton shirt, and his light jacket. He then went to the kitchen to wipe down the counters one more time. Sean was a fastidious cleaner—he liked everything neat and clean and he kept the apartment in immaculate condition at all times, yet he always felt he needed to clean some more. He felt he did his best thinking while cleaning, and it became a habit; to think meant to clean something, and by the looks of the apartment, he had been doing a lot of thinking.

Sean finished the counter, turned to leave, and then noticed the cell phone resting on the microwave oven. He grabbed it and browsed through the missed calls. Three of them were from Coleman. He'd called at eight o'clock, at nine, and then his last call was at ten. He'd waited exactly one hour between each call. Sean felt a fresh pang of guilt as he began to listen to his messages. The first was as expected, "Sorry I missed you, will call again at nine." The second started to get an edge: "Hope you are okay, call me when you get this message. If not I will call again at ten." The last was pissed: "Obviously you are not taking my calls for some reason. If I did anything to upset you, I'm sorry. Please call me." The last was stated firmly. He didn't call after that. Without thinking it through, Sean dialed Coleman's number, and he answered immediately.

"Hello, Sean. I hope you aren't canceling on me." That edge was there again, almost a dare to try and renege.

"No, I just listened to my messages, and I wanted to apologize again." Sean took a deep breath. "I will carry this thing from now on."

"I would appreciate that. I will see you in a few minutes."

"Would you like me to meet you out front?" Sean asked.

"No, I'll pick you up at your apartment," Coleman declared.

"Yes, sir." Sean hung up before Coleman could comment on the "sir."

Coleman arrived at seven o'clock sharp and found Sean anxiously awaiting his arrival, although he tried to look casual and relaxed. Coleman appreciated the fact that he seemed excited to see him.

Sean invited him in, and he accepted. He was dressed similar to Sean, in jeans and a white pullover with a light leather jacket. Even casual, this guy was commanding in how he walked and the way he looked at you. Sean glanced away and offered him coffee or juice.

"No, thank you. I thought we would do dinner and then a movie." Coleman advanced on him and grabbed his jacket from the chair, then helped him put it on.

No one had ever helped him put his jacket on before, and suddenly, he felt quite special.

Once they were in Coleman's car and on their way, Coleman began asking a few prying questions. Sean was very private and had a tendency to not share unless asked specifically for answers, and even then didn't go too far into the details.

"So, did you have any missed calls besides me?"

"Yes, several. I've started carrying it now." He pulled the cell phone out of his back pocket as proof.

"You don't have to carry it all the time," Coleman told him and held out his hand.

Sean put the phone in his hand, and Coleman deposited it in the storage area between the seats. Sean smiled and said, "There— no unwanted interruptions."

"Who called you? Anyone I know?" Coleman was probing to find out if it was Weir.

"Brittany called, and also Professor Weir. He didn't leave a message, so I didn't call him back." Sean hurried with his answers. He didn't like discussing either Brittany or Weir with Coleman.

"How did she get your number so fast? Are you and Brittany close?"

Sean started to laugh. "She got it from Professor Weir and no, not at all. She hates my guts."

"Why?"

"Because I exceeded her grade point average by .028. She is very touchy about grades." Sean continued to laugh. The idea of anyone thinking the two of them were friends was ludicrous.

"Why would she call you?" Coleman had begun to surmise that the call had been a hateful one, and he wanted clarification.

"She told me her brother Adam was in town visiting her for a week or so and wanted to know if I wanted to get together with them." This wasn't the complete truth, but Sean didn't want to get Brittany into trouble. Actually, she had said that if he continued screwing with her life, she would make sure Sean got together with her brother, who was in town. It was a threat, but like all of Brittany's threats, he took it as hollow.

Coleman cocked his eyebrow at him but did not question him further on that point. He had a hunch Sean wasn't being completely honest, but he let it go for now. "What about Weir? What could he possibly be calling you for? You reported on Sunday, didn't you?"

"Yes, and I'm not required to report again until next Sunday. Maybe he is concerned about my placement."

"For a twenty-three-year-old man who has lived on his own for the past two years, you are very naïve when it comes to people and their behavioral motives." Coleman decided to get his feelings out in the open as far as Weir was concerned.

"What do you mean?" Sean turned to look at him with his eyebrows knitted together. He didn't like being referred to as naïve.

"Professor Weir has designs on you," Coleman stated flatly.

"He has never given me that impression." Sean searched his memory for any indicators but came up empty.

"I've spoken with him regarding you on a couple of occasions, and believe me, Sean, his interest in you and your future is not completely platonic." Coleman turned to look at Sean sitting next to him and saw confusion and thoughtfulness cross his face.

"That is… very uncomfortable… to think about. I hope you're wrong." Sean fell silent until they reached the restaurant.

Coleman ordered for them both, but he asked Sean's permission first. He ordered steak and potatoes with a salad and, of course, pie for dessert. Dinner was elegant and delicious. They spoke of work and the experiences that Sean was getting and then veered into a more personal direction once again.

"Are you seeing anyone, Sean?" Coleman asked between sips of wine.

"No, my last relationship ended quite some time ago." Sean tensed up a bit, and Coleman sensed it.

"I have had quite a few men in my life." Coleman decided to share, considering he was asking so much of Sean. "I tend to keep things shallow. I have never had a… so-called relationship. I have never had room or made room for anyone long-term. I have tried on occasion to maintain a friendship with them, but that has proven to be impossible. Currently, I am not seeing anyone." Coleman riveted him with his gaze and noticed that Sean was doing the same.

Sean's mind was reeling, trying to understand what Coleman was saying and why he was saying it. Was he warning him off? Was he saying, "Don't even think I'm going to care about you?" Was he preparing him to be used and tossed aside like all of his other purported men? Sean suddenly felt slightly nauseous. He continued to stare at Coleman, feeling like he was seeing him for who he really was. This was the man everyone had described. He was admitting he was shallow, heartless, and fickle. Sean tore his eyes away and glanced nervously around the room.

Coleman abruptly reached over and covered Sean's hand with his own. "You have nothing to fear from me." He wasn't sure why he made that statement, but he knew Sean was suddenly troubled; he could feel it. Sean nodded but said nothing.

Sean frantically tried to come up with a subject to talk about other than the current one. He didn't want to hear any more of Coleman's history with regard to his conquests. "Which movie are we going to see?" It was a lame attempt, but it worked.

Coleman said thoughtfully, "We can decide when we get there." Coleman studied Sean as he sat there looking more uncomfortable than he'd seen him since the day they'd made their initial introductions. The remainder of the evening was stiff and stilted. The movie, although interesting, failed to capture Coleman's attention. All he could focus on was how far away Sean seemed. He was sitting next to him and holding his hand, but he wasn't there.

During their walk back to the car, Coleman abruptly asked, "Do you still love me, Sean?"

Sean turned to look at him, shocked by what he'd said, and waited for the punch line.

Coleman smiled, but it wasn't a confident or lighthearted smile. It was a smile that asked for understanding. "Last weekend you told me three or four times that you loved me. I miss hearing it."

Sean broke into a huge smile. He felt a subtle vibe of vulnerability in Coleman, and he liked it. He squeezed Coleman's hand and said with a fake alcoholic slur, "I love you, man."

That innocent declaration elicited a smile from Coleman that was both poignant and tender. He let go of Sean's hand and pulled him in for a big bear hug and a quick peck on the cheek. "I love you too, man," he said, mimicking Sean's feigned alcoholic tone. The remainder of the evening was lighter and so enjoyable that Coleman dreaded the moment he'd have to say good night.

They walked for a while and talked, then had hot chocolate at Sean's apartment and talked some more. When the time came for him to leave, Coleman hesitated and made excuses until finally, he grabbed his coat and headed for the door. Sean followed him to the door. Before leaving, Coleman turned, took Sean in his arms, and kissed him.

It wasn't the deep, sensuous kiss of last Sunday, but it was very good. It felt like Coleman cared for him, or so Sean thought. But he had to keep his head. He remembered the things Coleman had said during dinner and how casual he was about the men in his life and how easily they came and went. Nothing here was meant to be permanent; it was a matter of time before Coleman moved on to the next guy. *Stay grounded*, Sean coached himself.

"I'm going out of town for a couple of days. May I call you on Sunday?" Coleman paused in the doorway and waited for an answer.

"Of course. I will definitely keep the phone with me." Sean smiled, and Coleman reached out and kissed him again, harder. He acted as if he really didn't want to leave, but Sean assumed he was misreading the signals. Coleman had better things to do with his time than hang around with him.

Coleman released him then and said good night.

SEVEN

COLEMAN met with Jason the following morning to discuss a case that was taking them out of town, nailing down the details and the intended approach. Jason had been working on the case since the beginning, but now felt it would serve the client better if he passed it on to one of the other partners because of a possible perceived conflict of interest. After they finished, Jason and Coleman discussed more personal topics, and finally, Jason ventured to ask a few poignant questions regarding Sean, just out of curiosity. The moment Sean's name was mentioned, Coleman's eyes lit up, and a smile spread across his face.

"He is the sweetest, most interesting, most enjoyable individual I have ever gone out with," Coleman declared to a shocked Jason.

"Wow, that sounds serious." Jason simply stared at him and waited for more. "Are the sentiments mutual?" he asked.

"He couldn't stand to even be around me at first, but now he simply doesn't trust me," Coleman said with a small smile. "I have a long way to go yet, but he's worth it."

Jason laughed. "This is so unlike you. But I'm happy for you."

"Oh, I don't know what the longevity of this relationship will be, but I plan on enjoying it while it lasts." Coleman's smile faded as he contemplated his words.

"You plan on kicking him to the curb when you're finished with him like every other guy in your life, I suppose," Jason said as he was about to leave. "But this is the most interested I've ever seen you; it's refreshing, even if it is temporary." With that, he left the office.

Coleman pulled out his phone and immediately dialed. "Hello, Sean."

"Hey, good to hear from you," Sean answered. "Thought you were going out of town, and I wouldn't hear from you till Sunday?"

"I was suddenly thinking of you and needed to hear your voice." Coleman was not joking. The sound of Sean's voice relaxed him and took his mind off what Jason had said. "Last night, when I was telling you about some of my previous relationships, I later felt that perhaps I had been rather insensitive. I'm sorry if you were made to feel uncomfortable, and I want to add that, yes, I have known many men, but I have never known anyone like you." Coleman hoped Sean would understand. Last night after he'd gotten home, he'd gone over the evening in his mind, trying to figure out what had put Sean off, and it came to him that the "many men" statement probably sounded a bit scary.

"Thank you," Sean answered and then added, "You're pretty special too."

Coleman laughed and thanked him for the support. "I'll call you on Sunday… or maybe sooner."

Sean kept busy the rest of the day in order to keep thoughts of Coleman as far from his mind as possible. Ed invited him to dinner at his home, and Sean couldn't think of a better way to spend a Friday night. It was the first time he was able to spend time away from work with Ed, and he took advantage of it. They sat in Ed's living room and had drinks after dinner and talked. It became obvious to Sean that Ed had a lot he wanted to discuss with him.

Ed made the opening statement. "Mr. West appears to have taken an interest in you, Sean."

"He has been very good to me," Sean answered carefully.

Ed leaned forward in his chair and held Sean's gaze as he continued. "As you know, I have worked for Coleman West for the past five years." Sean nodded. "During that time I have seen him in the company of... many... men." He paused in case Sean wanted to say something, but he remained quiet. "Most of them understood the score—look good, be available, and go away when it is over. He abhors those who don't know enough to disappear when he is finished with them and try to hang on or use emotional blackmail to hold onto him." Ed shook his head and glanced away for a moment, as if gathering his thoughts before continuing. "He can be very unpleasant, to put it mildly. I've seen him look at a former lover like a piece of trash. I've seen him treat a former lover worse. Those who don't understand how he is end up very badly hurt. I'm telling you all of this because I don't want you to be one of them."

Ed hadn't told him anything that he didn't already know, or at least suspect, but hearing it stated so clearly by someone who obviously knew him was chilling. "We aren't lovers, sir," Sean said very quietly.

"You will be if Coleman has anything to say about it. He isn't nice without a reason, Sean—he wants something from you."

"I know, but I want something from him too." Sean looked at him squarely as he continued. "I'm not deluding myself, sir. I know who he is, and I know to expect nothing from him, emotionally speaking. But all I want is for him to know me and to accept me. He wrote the most terrible things about me when he rejected my application. He didn't know me at all and yet made malicious assumptions based on nothing. I want him to accept and appreciate who I am."

"That's a tall order, son. For Coleman West, acceptance and appreciation are almost as foreign as love." Ed smiled and Sean reciprocated.

"I'll be careful."

"You do that."

COLEMAN arrived in Minneapolis early and concluded his business by early evening. He was invited to dinner but begged off, complaining of fatigue and an early day tomorrow. Actually, his reasons for going back to the hotel were to have time to go over the contract for tomorrow and call Sean. Coleman had thought about him off and on all day and wondered if Sean had been thinking about him. He chastised himself for behaving like a thirteen-year-old girl, but still, he wanted to know.

He called Sean on the apartment line first, assuming he would be at home, but when he didn't answer, he followed up with a call on the cell. Sean answered after three rings.

"Doing anything interesting?" Coleman asked in an attempt to find out where he was.

"Mr. Murray invited me to dinner, and we are just finishing up," Sean explained.

"I won't keep you, then. Call me when you get home, okay?" He was unsure how he felt about Sean's evening with Ed. Part of him was jealous of anyone else getting close to Sean, although he appreciated Ed being there for him.

Sean agreed to call him as soon as he returned to the apartment, then asked how his trip was going. Coleman told him all was fine and he would definitely be home Sunday.

Ed just looked at him with that all-knowing expression that said, "You know he wants you."

Sean hunched his shoulders and said, "I know the score. Don't worry about me."

Sean returned to the apartment around ten and called Coleman as soon as he got settled in the living room with a cup of hot tea. They talked on a variety of subjects, including the weather in Minneapolis, and then settled into more personal issues, as always.

"Are you satisfied with your experience at the law firm so far?" Coleman asked

"Yes, I'm getting some practical experience, and Mr. Murray includes me in most of his court cases. I am very satisfied." Sean held fast to his desire to remain where he was. Coleman hadn't pushed him to change supervisors, but Sean was feeling that the conversation might lead in that direction.

"I have some information on local art schools and some intern opportunities with a couple of museums and marketing firms. I'd like to talk to you about them when I return. I know you value your legal-assistant certification, but it wouldn't hurt to at least give these possibilities a look." Coleman was planning on finding a way to keep Sean in Chicago following the completion of his internship. Art school or another internship would make that possible. He didn't tell Sean that, but he planned on continuing to set the groundwork for him to go forward with his art.

"I haven't made any decisions in that regard yet, but I will certainly look at any information you have." Sean wasn't keen on art school because he could not afford it right now and did not want to add to his debt. As far as another internship, he could not afford that, either, but he didn't want to get into that right now. He appreciated Coleman's interest in his career and his apparent belief in his art, but he had to stick with the legal-assistant certification for now and look at art later in his life. He needed to get settled, get a job, and get on with his life.

Coleman kept him on the phone talking until well after midnight. Sean had never talked on the phone that long in his life. What he didn't realize was that Coleman, too, had never held a conversation that long that wasn't work-related.

Sean spent Saturday in the park, drawing and soaking up some Chicago culture. He hadn't had the time or energy to take in much of the Chicago lifestyle before. Now that he was in the heart of downtown, thanks to Coleman and his sense of guilt, it was a pleasure to walk and draw and experience the town.

He was in the park by the fountain, having a hot dog and chips, when someone came up beside him and sat down. To his disgust, it was Brittany.

"So, not with your boyfriend today," she commented snicely. "He tired of you already?"

"Would you please leave?" Sean said as he continued with his lunch. He did not look at her as he spoke.

"You're the one who will be leaving. He will finish with you, and then we'll see who has the last laugh. I can't believe that he is satisfied with a lowlife like you anyway." She just kept poking.

"Are you still here?" He turned to look at her briefly and then glanced away.

She began to get angry and leaned into him as she continued her verbal agitation. "If you get in my way, I swear my brother will find you and rearrange your face."

"Bring it on," was all he said, and he got up and walked away.

Until Brittany came along, he'd been enjoying his day, but after her attack he decided to go home and watch some television or maybe read a book. To his complete surprise, Coleman called him on the apartment phone at eight thirty. His contact over the past few days had been nice. It seemed to Sean as if he did like talking to him. Coleman told him about his day and explained some of the case to him as if he were speaking to an equal. He even asked Sean's opinion on a couple of points. Sean carefully considered the questions and give very thoughtful answers. Perhaps he was being tested, and his answers, if not well thought out, would be used against him.

"Sean, why don't you trust me?" Coleman asked out of left field. It had nothing to do with the subject they were discussing but Coleman could feel that Sean was being so careful with his words.

He longed for Sean to completely let go with his opinions instead of the dribs and drabs of actual truth that he offered.

"You're Coleman West—you own the firm, you have the power to ruin me with the stroke of a pen, and you ask why I have trust issues." Sean was completely honest but within reason.

"Good point," Coleman admitted with humor around the edges of his tone. "I know my reputation precedes me and therefore it may be difficult for you to believe what I say now. But with that being said, I have never hurt anyone who didn't have it coming, as far as I was concerned, anyway. I have never ruined anyone who didn't need to be ruined, and any time that I have made a mistake, I apologize and make restitution. I will not give you trouble either personal or professional, no matter what you say to me, and on that you have my word." Coleman was sincere when he said he would never hurt him. Sean was a good man. Anything he said or did would come from a place of truth and honor, and Coleman knew that for a fact.

Sean decided to test the new openness. "Why has Mr. Murray never gotten above the third floor?"

"Up until you and your circumstances came along, I never really had a clear, full picture of who Ed Murray is." Coleman was again impressed that Sean would think about Ed before himself. "Since then, I have come to understand and appreciate him. You can be assured that Ed's future in the firm will be upward." Coleman recognized Ed's loyalty and dedication to the firm and to Sean. Ed sounded like someone who could be depended on no matter what the situation. Coleman needed employees like that, and he only wished he'd discovered that sooner. Ed had been with the firm for five years and Coleman was only now getting to know him.

"Do you plan to reprimand Mr. Murray for taking me as an intern?" Sean asked. It had been nagging at him for a while that even if Coleman didn't punish Ed, he would very likely wait until the internship ended and then make an example of Ed.

"I will do nothing against Ed; you have my word on that too." Coleman knew Ed's behavior was neither malicious nor underhanded. Ed had meant him no disrespect by accepting Sean; he simply saw someone being mistreated and tried to rectify the matter.

"Thank you." Sean did not pursue any further questions. Instead, they talked about Sean's art career, and he mentioned that he'd done some sketching in the park earlier. He didn't mention his run-in with Brittany. Coleman asked to see the sketches when he returned the next day, and Sean agreed.

"I'll be back tomorrow afternoon, and I will call you," Coleman announced. "Good night, Sean, see you tomorrow."

"Good night, Coleman," Sean answered carefully, still not comfortable with his name.

It was still early, so Sean decided to go for a walk. There was a small café just down the street that served excellent coffee. He remembered to take the cell phone with him, just in case.

JASON WEINTAUB had accompanied Coleman on his trip and knocked on his door just after he'd hung up from Sean.

"Come in." Coleman ushered him in and offered him a drink.

"No, thank you. I just stopped by to see if you wanted to go to the Attic Room. I hear it is the number-one hot spot in the area. I plan on checking it out." Jason was dressed in his best out-on-the-town outfit—jeans, white cotton shirt, and leather jacket. Everything about him said well-off, out-of-town business man, and that was exactly what he was shooting for. His look showed he was looking for something temporary, yet exciting.

"Sure, why not." Coleman grabbed his coat and met him at the door. He was still wearing his suit but decided it would do. He didn't feel like taking the time to change.

"Exactly, why not," Jason agreed, and together they headed for the Attic Room.

The nightclub was full and noisy, and Jason was in his element. Coleman, on the other hand, realized quickly that he probably should have stayed at the hotel. Several men approached him, but none were made welcome.

"What's wrong with you?" Jason asked. "That last guy was hot as hell. I would have gone after him myself if I were gay."

"Be my guest." Coleman laughed at his friend. "I'm just tired, I guess. Sorry."

He ended up staying for another hour and then begged off to return to the hotel. "You know you'll have more fun without me," he told Jason, who agreed.

On the way back to the hotel, he began to ponder why he was not feeling in the partying mood and decided it was definitely Sean. He began to consider how he would feel if he thought Sean was at a place like the Attic Room while Coleman was in Minneapolis. The thought brought anger and jealousy. He needed to see Sean tomorrow.

Coleman checked out of the hotel and arranged a flight back to Chicago that evening. Staying another night didn't seem necessary. He left a message for Jason, telling him that he wanted him to do the presentation on Sunday, and explained his departure.

Sean returned to his apartment by eleven, pulled out his sketches from that afternoon, and began to fine-tune them. Coleman had said he wanted to see them when he returned tomorrow, and Sean wanted them to be perfect before he saw them.

The doorbell rang at nine thirty the next morning. Sean was up and preparing pancakes and bacon for breakfast, so he set his spatula aside, wiped his hands, and went to the door.

"Hey, you're awful early. Thought you weren't leaving Minneapolis till this afternoon?" Sean graciously led Coleman in and took his jacket. "I'm making breakfast—would you like to join me?"

"Love to." Coleman took Sean's hand, pulled him toward him, and gave him a gentle, affectionate kiss. "Good morning."

Sean smiled and motioned for him to follow him to the kitchen, where he seated Coleman at a small table overlooking the courtyard. Sean brought him a cup of coffee, then went back to making pancakes.

Coleman sipped his coffee and watched as Sean prepared and served him a breakfast of pancakes with syrup and crisp bacon. This was the second meal Sean had prepared for him. No one in his past had ever taken the time to prepare anything for him. No one in any of his relationships had so much as poured him a cup of coffee. Sean treated him like he was special but also like he was a friend. Sean was used to taking care of himself and his mother, so it was probably natural that he took care of Coleman too. It made Coleman smile and left him with a warmth that was indescribable.

During breakfast, Coleman gave Sean the information regarding local art schools and internship opportunities. "Look them over and tell me what you think."

Sean leafed through the school pamphlets and was impressed by what they had to offer. He wasn't sure how to state that he could not afford more school right now. He continued to eat and read as he tried to come up with the words.

"I don't feel that I am prepared to continue with more school at this time. I want to keep all of this information, but I can't go in a different direction so soon. I want to complete the legal studies program and work for a few years before deciding on my next move." Sean hoped he'd said it clear enough without sounding poor.

"Are you saying you can't afford it?" Coleman cut to the chase.

"Not now. I have a lot of student loans, and I want to get them under control before I start adding to my debt." Sean was honest without sounding pathetic, at least he hoped.

"What about the internship?"

"I need to get a job."

"Why?"

"I'm twenty-three. I need to get settled."

"You're twenty-three, you have time. If art is your dream, don't let this opportunity pass you by." Coleman pressed hard for an agreement. He understood Sean's hesitance with regard to the debt, but the internship was paid, and Coleman would continue to provide him with an apartment. The internship was a three-month placement, and Coleman wanted the extra time with Sean. He wasn't sure what he wanted in the end, but for now he knew he wanted, no, *needed* more time. "Apply for the placement now, and make your decision at the end of your internship with me."

"Okay, I will do that." Sean saw no harm in applying. "Maybe you could give me a few pointers on what not to include in an internship application, considering you rejected mine." Sean couldn't help the jab.

Coleman dropped his fork and jumped to his feet. He grabbed Sean's hand and brought him to his feet. Coleman led him into the living room. "We're going to have this out right now, right here. Go ahead say whatever you need to get it all out of your system. I've had enough of the snarky remarks, so what's on your mind, Sean?" He was angry. He'd bent over backward trying to make things right with Sean, and he still took shots at him over the application. What did he want? "What do you want from me? What do you want me to say?" Coleman was nearly yelling and was still holding Sean by the shoulders and peering down at him intimidatingly.

"You've never been clear about why you rejected me. You've never told me what was in my application that made you toss it in the trash and write that letter." Sean looked up at him, meeting his gaze as he spoke.

Coleman softened his stance, let his hands travel down Sean's arms, and grasped both of his hands. He watched Sean and saw the hurt and confusion in his eyes as he explained. "I read that you had quit school and assumed it was because you couldn't cut it. I didn't read your explanation, just thought you lacked dedication. I also saw that you supported yourself by working at a nightclub. All that said to me was you are into drugs and alcohol. What I took from your application was that you are a dropout who is into drugs and alcohol." He paused and watched Sean, trying to gauge his comprehension.

Sean remained silent, processing his words, and found understanding. Finally he could see why he'd been rejected. Of course it wasn't fair, but the assumptions made were understandable. "All right," he said at last. "I get it now. It made me look pretty bad, but why didn't Professor Weir advise me to change it? I let him read it before I sent it to the law firm."

Coleman was relieved that Sean finally understood him but was now freshly concerned over the part that Weir might be playing in Sean's life. "I don't know," he stated softly. "As your professor, he should have helped you present yourself better."

"Do you think he set me up to be humiliated? He let me and everyone know that I had the highest marks, and I would get the placement with you. It wasn't until I was standing in front of everyone at that stupid dinner and placements were being announced and distributed that he made the announcement that Brittany got the placement with you. He let me fall flat on my face in front of everyone with no warning. It was one of the worst days of my life." Sean's eyes filled with tears, and he attempted to brush them away.

Coleman wrapped his arms around him and brought him up tight against him, cradling his head against his chest. "I'm sorry for the part I played in that spectacle." He placed a few kisses on the side of Sean's face and pressed him even closer.

"Why would he want to humiliate me? Then he got me a placement with Mr. Murray, which made him look like the good guy in all of this. I don't like Professor Weir very much right now."

"Better him than me." Coleman chuckled and then added, "Would you like me to go kick his ass? I will, you know, I'll do that for you."

Sean started to laugh. "Not right now, but maybe later."

"Anytime, Sean. Say the word and it is done." Coleman squeezed him again and gave him a long, deep kiss followed by an exploration of his neck and shoulder.

Sean pulled away carefully, not wanting to offend but also not wanting to get in too deep, too fast. This was still Coleman. He might be acting kind and considerate, but he was still the same man who, without another thought, had been willing to crush his career aspirations. Coleman had admitted he made snap judgments based on a few misplaced words. Sean told himself not to get too secure in his position as far as Coleman was concerned. Sean explained that he wanted to clean up the kitchen before they left.

Coleman released him and assisted in the kitchen cleanup. Then he suggested that Sean let him show him the sights of Chicago. They walked down around downtown, checking what Chicago had to offer. Parks, theaters, museums, skyscrapers—it was a feast for Sean's senses. He couldn't get enough of this town. Part of him would be genuinely sad to leave after the end of the internship. Deep down, he knew Coleman was also part of the reason he didn't want to leave.

They returned to Sean's apartment around three, and Sean showed Coleman the sketches he'd completed at the park the previous day. They discussed his art career further and Coleman pressed for a commitment to the internship.

Sean invited him to stay for dinner, and although Coleman ached to stay, he had a previous engagement he could not break. He left just after five, staying as long as possible and still giving himself enough time to get ready for the museum charity fund-raiser he was attending at seven. He had asked an acquaintance to accompany him, and they were going to meet at the museum at seven. He wished he could have brought Sean, but he'd invited Kevin weeks ago and it was too late to change that now. What would Sean think if he knew he was leaving in order to get ready for a date with another man? It was a date that had been set long before he ever met Sean. Would it bother him? Or did Sean not feel that their relationship was such that Coleman should give him preference? Unfortunately, Coleman believed the latter to be true.

Coleman pulled up in front of the museum and passed his keys to the valet. Kevin had called and said he would meet him inside around seven fifteen, but he was running late. Coleman told Kevin that if he was involved with something, he shouldn't feel he had to attend the gathering. Kevin said he was nearly finished getting ready and he would be there, not to worry. Actually, Coleman had been hoping Kevin would not be able to attend. After spending most of the last ten days with Sean, he felt strange escorting someone else to this function. He smiled at the memory of waking up next to Sean last weekend. The look on Sean's face when he turned and saw him there had been absolutely priceless. Then he remembered how Sean had felt in his arms and how he snuggled in close to him without hesitation. He felt a sudden stirring in his groin, so he decided to change the direction of his thoughts.

Upon entering the main room, he made his rounds among the guests and then took note of the pieces on display. The art was historic and priceless; he had not paid it much attention in the past, but now that Sean was in his life, he paid closer attention to the art around him. Sean was a very good artist, and with some specialized training he could be even better. He realized how quickly Sean had returned to his thoughts and smiled. Usually, this function was tedious and boring and he stayed only long enough to make an appearance. He had planned on taking Kevin back to his place and finishing the evening there, but those plans had changed. He couldn't think about anyone except Sean. Kevin meant nothing to him, never had. He was a good man in his own right, but Coleman was not into relationships, and Kevin's run had just about come to an end. It was time for Kevin to go away.

He thought again about Sean. Would he grow tired of Sean eventually? Would he want Sean to go away? Like before, this thought brought with it a deep-seated anxiety, a sense of subtle panic, even. Coleman took out his phone and brought up the picture of him and Sean he had taken in front of the furniture store. He was staring at the picture when Kevin came up beside him. Coleman quickly put the phone away and gave Kevin his attention.

"Sorry I'm late," Kevin said and took one of the glasses of champagne a waiter was offering from a tray.

"No problem," Coleman answered and turned his attention to the room.

Coleman gave him very little notice or consideration over the course of the evening, and it was just before ten when he announced he was leaving and said his good-byes to Kevin. Kevin assumed his cold treatment was due to his being late. You didn't arrive late if you were meeting Coleman West; he did not tolerate it. But the reason for Coleman's indifference was something else entirely; it was a young man who he had turned down when he had invited Coleman to dinner, a young man sitting alone in an apartment.

He wanted to stop and see Sean, but was it too late? Coleman began to analyze his feelings for Sean as he drove to his apartment. Never had he ever spent so much idle time with one person and enjoyed it so much. What was it about Sean that attracted him on so many levels? He was a handsome young man, but that wasn't it. Kevin was a handsome man too, but Coleman couldn't get away from him fast enough when he hoped to spend an hour or two with Sean. He had felt guilty about his condemning appraisal of Sean, but only after meeting him and feeling that immediate connection. He knew himself well enough that he would not have felt guilty if he hadn't felt attraction. No, it wasn't just guilt. It was something about Sean's eyes, in the way he stood, his sense of pride and dignity, and his personality and strength of character. Coleman realized that everything about Sean attracted him… the whole package.

He wanted to see him tonight, but would he look like a stalker if he showed up there at this hour? If he had a reason for being there, his presence would be accepted without question, but what was the reason? He searched for a plausible answer and finally decided that instead of sending his assistant Janet and her intern on a scheduled out-of-town business trip, he would go himself and take Sean. It would give him an opportunity to have Sean alone for a period of time in a very nonthreatening environment. It would appear to be strictly business. The trip was scheduled for eleven the next morning. He quickly called Janet, who was pleased to hear the news, since she would rather stay home with her family, and then he arranged for a flight as he made his way across town to give Sean the good news. He was extremely proud of himself for coming up with such a perfect plan so quickly

Sean was relaxing in front of the flat-screen television Coleman had purchased for the apartment when he heard a knock on his door. It was ten twenty-five, and he had no idea who could be at his door at this hour. As he approached the door, he assumed it was a neighbor or maybe the super, but was floored when he opened the door to Coleman. He was dressed in a tuxedo and overcoat, looking like he was on his way to a royal wedding or something. Every hair in place, he looked stunningly handsome, so much so that Sean just stood there and stared for a few moments.

"Wow, you look great," Sean said. He tore his gaze away and invited Coleman in.

"Thank you. You look pretty good too," Coleman teased as he proceeded to take off his overcoat, which Sean took and hung in the closet.

"I feel like I should go put on a tie." Sean looked down at his worn-out college tee and jeans and instantly felt inferior.

Coleman stared at him and said nothing for a while. His gaze seemed to burn right through him. Sean stood still and waited. The air was immediately charged and heavy. Without warning, Coleman stepped suddenly forward and grabbed him with a hand on each side of his head, pulling Sean to him as he brought his head up and kissed him, hard and exacting. It was like no other kiss Sean had ever experienced. It wasn't casual and it wasn't friendly; it was passionate and needy and hot. Sean caught his breath and held onto Coleman to steady himself with a hand on each side of his waist. He didn't understand what was happening and he didn't know what he should do or what was expected of him. Finally, he could hold back no longer and joined in the kiss to the point that he let his hands travel the length of Coleman's back, pressing himself to him and feeling every muscle, every inch of his torso. Coleman pushed his right hand upward and threaded his fingers through Sean's hair. He continued holding Sean tightly, as if he thought Sean might try to escape and he was not going to let him.

Coleman tore his lips away and started kissing his way along Sean's jaw, letting Sean take a few ragged breaths, and then he quickly returned to the kiss. He came back even deeper and more demanding, and Sean began to feel a rising panic. It formed first in the back of his mind, questioning why Coleman was kissing him like he desired him, and then burst forth as pure paranoia. Sean stiffened and drew back within Coleman's grip.

Coleman compensated by pulling him into his arms and slamming him up against him as he continued the kiss. He felt Sean pulling away but he couldn't let him go, not this time. He explored with his lips as he penetrated with his tongue. Sean tasted like ambrosia and felt like heaven.

Sean shifted as much as he could within the embrace. His mind was scrambling to understand as his body trembled with the desire stirring in his veins. He wanted Coleman badly but couldn't let himself go. He had to maintain as much control as his body and mind could pull together. A deep groan escaped Sean's throat, and Coleman slid one hand down Sean's body, cupped his behind, and press Sean into him, seductively grinding against him. He moved Sean up against the wall behind them and used the firm surface to his advantage. The grinding and kissing continued at an alarming intensity. Coleman ran his hand down Sean's side to rest momentarily on his hip before slipping lower to massage Sean's crotch with his palm. He felt Sean groan into his mouth and move his hips in rhythm with Coleman's hand.

"Damn," Coleman moaned painfully. "Sean, oh, sweetheart." His words were gasped between pain-filled breaths. He sounded as if he were being tortured.

Sean reached up and grabbed ahold of Coleman with both hands on his upper arms and slammed against him even harder than he was already being pressed. He couldn't seem to get close enough or get enough pressure where he so desperately needed it.

Coleman was on fire. He felt Sean's need, his desire, and it mirrored his own. All thought of intern, supervisor, placement, and proper conduct vanished into the inferno raging in his veins.

A sudden thought from somewhere outside of himself hit Sean like a punch in the gut, and he began pulling away forcefully. If this continued in the direction it was headed, he would end up in bed with Coleman. He was a poor kid from the wrong side of the tracks, not someone Coleman would ever consider as a romantic partner. There was no future in what was happening between them. Coleman would see him as nothing but a booty call, a whore. That thought caused Sean to actually fight for his freedom and release.

Coleman let him go immediately and backed away, overwhelmed with a sense of panic that he had gone too far. "I'm sorry." The words came out with a tremor in his voice. "I didn't mean to scare you." His gaze held Sean as firmly as his arms had previously.

Sean stood still, composing himself and catching his breath. "I won't be used," he whispered and did not make eye contact with Coleman. "If this is why you let me stay, then I might as well go home. I don't sleep around. Like I told you before, I have had only one serious relationship in my life, and that ended over two years ago." He fell silent and waited for Coleman to tell him to clear out and get lost.

"Why did it end?" Coleman needed to talk, and he latched onto anything to get Sean talking. He was on the edge of losing Sean, and he had to be very careful. He watched his every movement, every nuance of emotion that crossed his face. He had to fix this; he had to make this right.

"As it turned out our values were very different." Sean ran his hand through his hair in a nervous gesture. "He left me for someone more in tune with his life goals." He looked around the room, looking for somewhere to rest his gaze. He couldn't look at

Coleman, who was probably laughing, probably turning his back on him, probably leaving. The discomfort was thick and hanging in the air. Something needed to be said.

Coleman took a tentative step toward him with his hand out. "I apologize. It was supposed to be just a kiss. I didn't mean to offend you. I didn't mean to make you feel used. That was never my intent. You are a very desirable man. I got carried away, and again, I apologize."

Sean looked at his hand and listened to his words. Slowly, he reached out and took Coleman's hand, holding it loosely at first and then gripping it firmly as he smiled and finally made eye contact. Coleman relaxed upon seeing him smile. "I think very highly of you, Sean, and I truly want for us to be friends. I let you stay because I like you, and you deserved the placement." He held firmly to Sean's hand and looked at Sean's face for a long time, reading and gauging every reaction. "How about I go back out into the hall and knock and we start this evening all over again." Coleman gave a weak smile and looked at Sean.

Sean laughed and that terrible mood was broken, thank God. They were back, the connection was secure, and Coleman was so relieved he too started to laugh.

"Would you like a cup of tea?" Sean asked.

"Yes, I would love a cup of tea." He watched as Sean disappeared into the kitchen. He took a deep breath and thanked God for the second chance, or was this a third chance? He wasn't sure, but he did know that God was being good to him. Sean returned to the room with his tea moments later, and they sat in the living room. Coleman took the sofa and Sean sat in the chair.

"I am going to visit one of our larger clients tomorrow. He lives on a secluded estate outside of Cleveland, on the water." Coleman took a sip of his tea and then set it on the end table by the sofa and continued. "That was the original reason I stopped by." He gave Sean a bleak smile. "I need an assistant to come with me, and I would like for you to fill that position." Sean remained quiet, knowing there was more to the request. "We will fly out tomorrow and will be staying in the area for a couple of days, during which time we will be reviewing his case." Coleman watched him closely. "We will have separate rooms," he added.

Sean smiled, a little embarrassed. "My only concern is Mr. Murray."

"He will be fine. If you would like, I could assign Ms. Saunders to him for the week," Coleman suggested and then was taken aback by the expression on Sean's face. "What?" he automatically asked for clarification.

"I couldn't do that to Brittany. She got the prize position when you rejected me, and she played it for all it was worth. I couldn't embarrass her by having her cover my position as I fly off with the boss." Sean dropped his gaze to his tea cup.

"Did she worry about embarrassing you when she took your position?" Coleman asked matter-of-factly.

"No, she rubbed it in… with salt. But I'm not Brittany, and I don't treat people like that." Sean hoped he wasn't sounding weak.

"Okay, I won't reassign Ms. Saunders, but you are coming with me, so be ready." Coleman finished his tea and stood up. He wanted to go over to Sean, take his hand, and bring him to his feet and then kiss him, but considering how the visit had started, that was probably not a good idea.

Sean stood up and approached Coleman. "I appreciate the opportunity to work with you. Thank you for choosing me for this trip."

"You're very formal, Sean," Coleman said and took a step closer to him. "You don't have to be. I want to give you a good work experience. It is the least I can do, considering what I've put you through." Coleman took another careful step toward him, looked at Sean squarely, and decided to give him some truth. "You are a very attractive man, and if our circumstances were different— that is, if you weren't one of the law firm's interns—I would be pursuing you full-on. I wouldn't take no for an answer. Just so you know, when you finish this placement, I am coming for you. Until then, I will respect your need for space, and I will try to control myself, but no promises." Coleman extended his hand. He needed to tell Sean how he felt and he needed to keep the door open for a relationship.

Sean was shocked by his declaration. He searched his face waiting for the "gotcha," the "I had you going, didn't I?" statement, but Coleman seemed serious.

"Are you serious?" He couldn't believe what he had just heard.

"As a heart attack." Coleman smiled grimly with his hand still outstretched, waiting.

"I'm flattered." It was all Sean could think of to say as he took Coleman's hand.

"You should be," Coleman teased. "I'm a good catch."

"I'll keep that in mind." Sean decided to lighten up and see how it was received, so he stepped closer, reached up, and gave Coleman a kiss. Coleman leaned into it as soon as he registered what Sean was going to do. He was ecstatic and took Sean's lips in a gentle caress, letting Sean take control. "I'll be ready," Coleman told him after the kiss ended. Coleman stared at him again in that all-consuming way that he had.

"See you tomorrow." Coleman's words and his eyes were having separate conversations. His words were cordial, but his gaze was penetrating, seeing what was inside him. Coleman grabbed his coat and quickly left the apartment.

Shortly after Coleman left, Sean went into the kitchen to wipe down the counters. *He can't be serious even though he said that he was. Coleman would not waste his time with someone like me. He could have a hundred young guys like me if he wanted them. Why pick me?* He kept thinking and was still digging for what must be the real reason when his cell phone rang. It surprised him because he rarely received calls at this time of night. He went over to it and stared at the caller ID. It was Brittany Saunders. He answered with hesitation, not sure why she would be calling him. They were not friends and they did not have conversations.

"Hello," he stated finally.

"Sean Robbins, you little piece of shit!" she exploded.

"You're such a refined young lady," he shot back sarcastically.

"How dare you insinuate yourself in with Mr. West and take my position? I'm going to destroy you." Her threats were always without real substance, but she usually put a lot of feeling into the verbal aspect of it.

"What position did I take?" He remained calm, and it irritated her to no end, as he had known it would.

"Mrs. Hendricks and I were supposed to go to Cleveland this week. She just called me and canceled because Mr. West and his intern, Sean, are going. You little piece of useless garbage." She was screaming now.

"Them's the breaks, Brittany. You win some, and you lose some. This one you lose." He felt rather satisfied.

"He's only taking you because it is an overnighter, and he probably thinks that you will be willing to do him, which you will you little whore." She wanted to hear him squirm; she wanted him to hurt.

He started to laugh. "Are you even listening to yourself?" He continued to laugh. "He dates the best in society, haven't you paid attention to the gossip? He doesn't do pieces of shit, useless garbage, or little whores." He snorted as he hung up on her. Her conversation had upset him, but he would not let her know that. Little did she know that if Sean had been willing, Coleman would probably be doing him right now. But maybe not. Maybe he'd been testing the water, that's all; maybe he wasn't ready to dive in

EIGHT

THE car arrived the next morning at nine sharp. Sean had packed his backpack with a set of dress clothes and a set of casuals and hoped that would be enough. He put all the necessary equipment into his messenger bag and headed out the door. Coleman was waiting for him on the sidewalk with a pleasant smile on his face.

"I'm going to have to get you a set of luggage." He took his backpack and stowed it in the trunk with his bags. They then sat together in the backseat as the driver took them to the airport. Coleman had chartered a private plane to take them to Cleveland, where they would be staying at the local Marriott. From there, they would hire a car to take them to the client's estate. Sean had never been on a private plane before and had only been on a regular passenger plane once. It was a very rich feeling. The plane had large seats with snacks and drinks and places to do your work. It was like a flying posh hotel room. Coleman was all business. He explained about the client, Jordan Bail, a banker from Chicago who was currently being accused of hiding assets during a divorce proceeding. He probably was, but that wasn't their concern. Their concern was representing the client to the best of their ability. Coleman explained this with care and a severe look.

"They pay us to do our jobs, not to be their conscience," he said when he noticed the look on Sean's face.

"Yes, sir."

"This is his fourth divorce and her third. Neither of them is innocent or unsophisticated in matters of matrimony. There are no victims here; keep that in mind." He glanced up from his paperwork to gauge Sean's acceptance.

"Yes, sir, I understand." Sean went back to reviewing the court papers Coleman had given him. It looked like Bail and his wife were both rather greedy and vindictive, although Bail had a point with regard to property acquired before the marriage. It looked like he had a very good case. Sean was surprised Coleman would follow this case personally, considering it looked like a slam dunk.

They arrived at the hotel and checked into their rooms. They had adjoining rooms, which made sense considering Sean was Coleman's assistant during this trip. They had to have easy access to each other. *It's just business*, he assured himself. The room was large and very comfortable. Sean was getting settled when there was a knock on the door between their rooms. He quickly went and opened it. He was instantly struck by the size and opulence of Coleman's room in comparison to his.

"Wow!" he stated as he looked around the room from the doorway. "I thought my room was something, but it's just the servant's quarters next to this place." He grinned. "Is that a living room?"

Coleman laughed at his excitement over a hotel room and invited him inside. He realized he was seeing everything with fresh eyes these days when he saw them with Sean.

"May I look around?" Sean asked.

"Help yourself." Coleman stood back and observed as Sean went from room to room.

The bedroom was separate from the rest of the hotel room and was set back so the windows looked out over the cityscape. *Very pretty*, Sean thought and wished he could do a few sketches from this vantage point. He stood there for some time, admiring the view.

"If you'd like to do some sketches from there, feel free." Coleman had read his mind. "Did you bring your sketchbook with you?"

Sean nodded. He turned back to the view, studying the layout as Coleman came up behind him. "Would you like room service or the restaurant for lunch?" Coleman broke into his thoughts.

"Whatever suits you, sir." Sean turned to regard him.

The way Sean constantly referred to him as "sir" was beginning to bother him. Coleman understood that a level of respect was necessary in a business relationship with a superior, but he didn't want Sean to call him "sir" when they were alone in his hotel room. It felt wrong.

"Sean, I know this is a lot to ask of you, but when we are alone, like now"—he looked around the room—"would you not call me 'sir'?"

"Mr. West?" Sean offered as a substitute.

"Try Coleman." He stared at Sean as he processed the request. "Just try it. Say it once," he urged. "Coleman. I want you to say my name. Coleman," Coleman continued to press good-naturedly.

"What if I screw up and forget and call you by name when I shouldn't. It could be embarrassing for you." Sean really didn't feel comfortable at this stage of their friendship, or relationship, or whatever it was, calling Coleman by his first name. He'd tried it once already and it felt awkward and disrespectful.

"You are too careful, it would never happen. Besides, I don't care if it does. Now say my name. I want to hear it." Coleman was not going to let it go.

"Coleman," Sean said clearly and maintained his gaze as he did so.

"That actually looked painful." Coleman smiled. "Try it again."

"Coleman!" Sean stated loud and clear.

"Better." Coleman enjoyed the sound of his name when it came from Sean's lips. It was going to be a long two days; so close, yet so far, he lamented. "Let's do room service. We can eat in here and review the case further. We meet with Bail at two thirty at his estate."

Sean nodded. He'd been close to saying, "Yes sir," but he caught himself in the nick of time.

Coleman ordered for both of them Cobb salad, iced tea, and pie. Remembering that Sean liked baked apples with ice cream, he ordered some for both of them. He wasn't much for dessert, but if Sean liked it, then it must be worth trying. Coleman asked Sean if he had any other requests, to which he quickly shook his head.

It was so nice being here with Coleman like this, like equals almost. Sean knew that it was not likely to persist once they returned to the law firm.

It was just past one when they headed toward the estate. Coleman had rented a Mercedes with a driver to take them there. Sean decided he could get used to this kind of life. He and Coleman sat in the back and discussed many things. Coleman was so relaxed today, Sean thought. It surprised Sean that he had used Coleman's first name. It was just in his thoughts, but it had come out rather naturally. Maybe he was making progress. He smiled to himself at his own ramblings. Coleman saw this and commented on it.

"What's so funny?" He casually reached over and laid his hand on Sean's knee.

"I was just thinking about being here with you and how unlikely it would have seemed two weeks ago. Life is really strange sometimes. But good," he added in case Coleman focused on the word "strange."

Coleman smiled and squeezed and patted his knee. He left his hand there throughout the drive, only removing it when they arrived at their destination.

The estate was massive. Sean had to school his features to stop his jaw from dropping open every time he turned a corner in the sprawling mansion. It had everything, including a standard-size theater, Olympic swimming pool, full-size bowling alley, a dining room that was larger than most restaurants he'd been in, and it went on and on. He noticed that Coleman paid attention to line, form, and structure. He wasn't impressed with the item; he was impressed with its construction. But unlike Sean, he was not the least bit obvious with his attention. Sean noticed because he was watching him and waiting for him to show any particular interest.

"The man loves his creature comforts," Coleman commented to Sean. "He also likes for people to be impressed by his possessions. You have made his day, Sean, I'm sure. He always has his butler greet the guests, and he watches by closed-circuit camera to see their reactions. You, with your wide-eyed amazement, made him very happy." Coleman came up behind Sean and slipped his arm around him as he was standing admiring a large oil painting on the wall.

"Wow, is all that I can say—wow," Sean tried to whisper.

The meeting lasted nearly four hours, during which Sean witnessed Coleman at his best in terms of legal expertise, gentle but firm people handling, and awesome interpersonal skills. Sean took notes for Coleman and for himself. He learned lessons that would serve him well in the future. Bail was a total ass, but Coleman treated him with respect and like shit at the same time. It was genius. In the end, Bail agreed to everything Coleman suggested or demanded. Sean wasn't sure which it was, since it came across as a suggestion but felt like a demand. Coleman was so subtle with his manipulation and control that Bail didn't even realize he was being controlled. Sean commented on this when they were leaving. Coleman just smiled.

That evening, Coleman took Sean to a very posh restaurant downtown, where they discussed Bail and the case, and then ventured into more personal subjects. Sean did not notice until later that Coleman had been leading the conversation in this direction from the start.

"Last night you mentioned that you have had one serious relationship in your life, and it ended two years ago," Coleman stated, and Sean nodded. "Did it end because you left the legal studies program and went home to care for your mother?" He had put two and two together last night, but sought verification.

Sean didn't answer immediately. He took a long drink from his wine glass before deciding what to say. "My mother was and is very important to me. If anyone ever asked me to choose between them and her, they are the losers." His explanation was cryptic, yet clear.

"You're very loyal to people you love," Coleman commented.

"I'm loyal to people that I trust and I love," Sean agreed.

"You didn't love this man?"

"Apparently not, and he did not love me." Cold, but again, very clear.

"Someone who loves you would not ask you to choose?" Coleman probed for clarity.

"They would not ask me to make an impossible choice that I could not live with later." Sean's tone was becoming clipped, so Coleman backed off.

"Have you had any relationships since this man?"

"No."

"Why not?"

"Not a deliberate action to cloister myself, if that is what you're thinking. I just haven't met anyone interesting or interested." Sean gave a weak smile and glanced around the room. These questions were beginning to wear on him. He feared he might say something that exposed too much.

Coleman stood up and gave Sean his hand, indicating for him to follow, which he did. There was a park surrounding the restaurant, and Coleman asked if he'd like to take a walk before going back to the hotel. Sean stated that a walk in the fresh night air would be very welcome. They spoke little throughout the walk, simply enjoying the other's company.

They made their way back to the hotel just after eleven, and Coleman invited Sean to his room for a drink before bed. Sean changed into his casual clothes—jeans and a light cotton T-shirt—before knocking on the adjoining door. He heard Coleman shout, "Come in, it's open."

Sean followed the voice to where Coleman stood. He was in the bedroom, looking out over the city from the window Sean had admired that morning. He had a drink in each hand. He gave one to Sean with a broad smile and said, "Just one for you tonight." The memory of last Saturday night came back Sean, and he blushed a bright red.

"I'll try to control myself," he answered and took the glass.

"Please don't," Coleman responded with a strange tone in his voice. Sean noticed that Coleman had also changed and was wearing thin, very worn jeans and a white shirt. "I'm glad you're here with me, Sean." He turned to regard him standing next to him at the window. "I find your perspective very refreshing and sometimes enlightening. What are your thoughts regarding the meeting today with Bail?"

"I didn't like Mr. Bail. He is a scared, rich man—not a very attractive quality."

"You find fear unattractive."

"His fear is unjustified, so yes, his fear makes him weak and vulnerable." Sean knew he had to explain further now that he had begun. "He is so selfish… he bases his worth on his possessions and fears the loss of even the smallest item. He acts like it will detract from him personally if someone is allowed to take something from him Do you understand what I'm saying?" Sean asked.

"Yes, and I agree. He values nothing except his possessions, and it puts him in a position of weakness. But he has worked hard for what he owns, and who are we to judge him on his values?" Coleman took a long sip and stared out the window. "I'm hardly the poster boy for proper living."

"What does that mean?" Sean decided to try to pry a little. "I think you could lose everything you own and still maintain who you are. You could be a fry cook in a diner and still be the same man you are now in every way that matters. You are not what you own."

Coleman turned to look at Sean again with a feeling of amazement. He felt as if he was looking at Sean for the first time. His gaze traveled over Sean from head to toe and back again. Sean continued to look out the window, unaware of the effect his words had on Coleman. Coleman set his drink on the side table and put his arm around Sean, drawing him up to his side.

Sean casually glanced over to look in Coleman's eyes and froze. There were tears in Coleman's eyes, not emotional flowing-down-your-face tears, but tears he was trying desperately to control.

Coleman took the drink from Sean's hand and placed it next to his on the table, never letting his eyes stray from Sean's. With his other hand, he cupped Sean's cheek as his eyes continued to bore into him. He wanted to say something but no words could convey what he was feeling at that moment. In two sentences, Sean had validated him, validated everything he was.

"What's wrong?" Sean asked softly, very concerned that he'd overstepped and said something that had upset him.

"Nothing… nothing at all. Everything is… perfect." His words were spoken very quietly as he slowly drew Sean into his arms and pressed him securely to his chest. He dropped his head so that his cheek was resting on the top of Sean's head. Sean put his arms around Coleman's waist and held him tightly, reciprocating an embrace of acceptance and need. He pressed his face into Coleman's chest and his senses were filled with his scent. He smelled better than anything on this earth—a mixture of musk and raw strength. It made Sean rub his face into him, drinking in the aroma as he moved his hands to span the expanse of Coleman's back, feeling the muscles twitch as he touched and explored.

Coleman dropped his head further in order to whisper hoarsely into his ear as he massaged his scalp and continued to press his head against his chest, binding Sean to him. "I want you... please, Sean." He knew he had said he would wait and he would keep his distance until after the summer session, but he was beyond human endurance. Desire had never been a tangible thing for him before. It had always been subtle and on the fringes of his schedule. It was something to enjoy during idle times but could be easily put away and denied if need be. That was not the case at present. Every fiber of his being was demanding satisfaction and release, and nothing short of Sean's absolute refusal would be able to stop him. "Please, Sean." He had to accept him; he had to want him. His thoughts were becoming frantic with his need to have Sean... now. Coleman's breath was shallow and labored as he continued his ministrations. "Don't you want me?" he implored and then let his lips trail from Sean's ear down his neck, craving more... yearning for more.

"I want you," Sean groaned into his chest where his face was pressed and his senses were consuming him. He didn't care what anyone thought; he didn't care if Coleman thought less of him after, all he knew was that he would not let this moment go. He wanted him more than anyone in his life. He had to have him, and he had to have him now.

Coleman registered his compliance and immediately thrust him onto the bed beside them and following him down, pinning him in place. He grabbed Sean's T-shirt and hauled it over his head and off in one fluid movement.

Sean was startled by the swiftness of the assault. He was off his feet, on the bed, and minus his shirt in less than five seconds. He caught his breath just in time for Coleman to capture his mouth in a kiss so passionate and erotic that he was instantly in full arousal. Sean groaned and shifted slightly to the left. His erection was pinned against Coleman's thigh and it was beginning to be painful. Just as quickly, Coleman adjusted so that he was planted firmly between Sean's thighs, all pressure now on the spot that needed it most, and he was taking full advantage of Sean's need to thrust. Coleman moved his hands to support the back of Sean's neck and angle him into the extremely forceful and wet kisses that were consuming him, while he used his hips to apply enough pressure to grind Sean into the bed.

Sean, overcome with the moment and not willing to resist, regardless of the cost, started to pull at Coleman's cotton shirt. He wanted it off; he wanted to see the man, feel the man. Coleman leaned back to give him better access and assisted Sean in removing his shirt. Soon they were both bare to the waist, and Coleman took the opportunity to explore. He held Sean's hands above his head while trailing wet kisses from his chin to his left shoulder, where he sucked and bit into the tender flesh, causing a distinct shudder and moan from Sean.

"Oh, Sean," Coleman groaned. "You are so beautiful." Coleman followed the statement by dipping lower and tasting just above Sean's navel. He swirled and licked the area before slipping his fingers inside the waistband of Sean's jeans, then working the snap open and the zipper down, revealing a pair of black boxer briefs. He never stopped or slowed his fingers' slow progression inside the briefs to free the hard length inside. Coleman gripped him firmly and began a slow pump as his lips continued their exploration of Sean's hip and stomach.

Sean thought his head was going to explode. Coleman of Coleman West and Associates was between his legs, jerking him off. It was beyond belief, beyond his wildest daydream, but t was real and it was happening to him. Just when he thought it couldn't get any better, Coleman dove lower and replaced his hand with his mouth. He took Sean completely, head to base, in one motion.

"Oh, baby, that feels amazing." The words were out of his mouth before he had a chance to censor them. Had he just called Coleman West "baby?" He would have stressed over it onger except for the sudden rush of euphoria pulsating from his crotch. "Coleman!" he burst out with pleasure.

Coleman slid his lips off for just a moment and caught Sean's gaze with a slight smile playing around his mouth and evident in his eyes. "I prefer 'baby'."

Sean felt the laughter vibrate as Coleman returned in earnest to his ministrations. Faster and faster he pumped until Sean was on the edge of screaming. The heat of his mouth and the suction he created was mind-blowing. Sean came with such force it made him jerk and stiffen beneath Coleman as he held his breath, unable to breathe through it. Coleman slid up his body to lay on him fully, looking down into his eyes. Sean did not speak; words weren't necessary. Coleman positioned himself back between Sean's legs and once again began to grind into him while staring into his eyes. Gradually, he moved to slip off Sean's jeans along with his own.

Sean continued to lay silent and simply stared at Coleman as he pressed up on his thighs, smoothing the skin under his palms. "You are a gorgeous young man," Coleman hissed through clenched teeth as he rose up on his knees, Sean's legs straddling him on either side. Coleman again ran his hands up the inside of Sean's thighs, pressing and spreading the tender flesh. Sean groaned and uttered excited sounds that were like words, but impossible to understand. Coleman smiled and continued toward his goal of complete satisfaction. He leaned over and grabbed the lube and condom that he'd placed on the nightstand earlier, in hopes of Sean's acquiescence. When he'd placed them there, sheer lust and need had spurred him on, but now he found himself overcome with real desire and passion, not the take-you-now-and-leave-you kind, but the I-want-to-discover-everything-about-you kind of passion. He didn't think on it too long before Sean began to squirm expectantly beneath him.

Sean knew what was coming, and he was apprehensive and excited at the same time. He hadn't had a lover in two years and hadn't been entered in that time. He knew there would be pain, but he also knew that Coleman was not a newbie. Coleman would most certainly give him an experience to remember, he assured himself when he felt the coolness of the lube as Coleman inserted first one finger and then a second. Coleman leaned over and took his lips in a tender, searching kiss that was more romantic than lustful and felt divine.

"I'm good, I'm ready, and it's okay." Sean panted the words he hoped would give Coleman the permission he seemed to be seeking. With a loud groan and a powerful thrust, Coleman entered completely and then paused for a moment, allowing Sean to adjust to the intrusion. Sean gasped and then relaxed as Coleman began a slow rhythm at first and then gradually picked up speed as his need seemed to consume him.

Coleman couldn't believe the feeling of being inside Sean. It was electric in its intensity, and overwhelming in the sense that his only desire was to please Sean. He wanted to give him the most, the best; he wanted him to call him sweetheart. "Sean, honey, talk to me," he whispered in a low, sexy growl that went straight to Sean's groin.

"You feel fantastic. This is incredible, you are incredible. Oh, baby, don't stop." Sean didn't even realize he'd called him baby again, although Coleman heard it and it pushed every button he had.

Within moments, Coleman was coming with an intensity he'd never before experienced. He simply held onto Sean and rode it out. Panting and gripping at Sean's shoulders for balance, he finally gave up and dropped down on top of him. "Baby, that was… beyond extraordinary," Coleman gasped out between labored breaths. He snuggled his face into Sean's shoulder and embraced him so tightly Sean could barely breathe, but he was not complaining.

Sean wrapped his arms around Coleman to hold and soothe him. "That was perfect." Sean was almost purring with satisfaction.

"You are perfect," Coleman corrected as he slid to the side in order to give Sean room to breathe but kept him within the circle of his arms and kept his face tucked into Sean's shoulder. He felt too good to move.

Coleman drew the comforter up to cover them both. He then pulled Sean back into his embrace and held him as he fell asleep. Coleman felt exhausted, full, and complete. Sean was his world at that moment; nothing else existed except the feel of his heartbeat against him and the warmth of his breath where it fanned against his throat. Would he feel like this in the morning? Or would he suddenly find his need had subsided and discard Sean, like he had so many others, now that he had tasted him? The thought brought a clenching in the pit of his stomach, anxiety, a sense of loss. He pushed the thought aside and gripped Sean tighter. Sean moaned in his sleep, and Coleman kissed his forehead and fell asleep beside him.

The ring was loud and persistent to the point that Sean woke abruptly and attempted to sit up. "My phone. Where's my phone?" He was groggy but awake. He started pulling away but was soon jerked back into place and pressed back down into the plush mattress beneath him by the weight of the man in bed with him.

"It's three in the morning; you don't have to answer your phone." Coleman gathered him in, snuggling his face into the crook of his neck again and placing a kiss there. "Go back to sleep, Sean." Sean wrapped his arms around him and did as he was told. When morning came, Coleman found himself lying in Sean's arms, his head on his chest and his arm draped over his torso. Sean was holding him as though he treasured him, loved him. Coleman drew back in order to look at Sean's face. When he did so, he saw that Sean was regarding him just as seriously and as deeply as he was him. Coleman wondered how long Sean had been lying there awake, staring at him. He looked contemplative; what was he thinking?

"I better go," Sean stated, and dropping his arms from around him, he made to get up, but Coleman remained where he was. He laid his head back on Sean's chest, which prevented Sean from moving. He put his arm back around Coleman and idly ran his fingers through his hair, pushing it back from his face.

"Stay," Coleman urged, because he did not want this moment to end. He'd never had anyone hold him like this. He felt safe, loved—cherished, even— and it was the greatest feeling of his life so far. He closed his eyes and lost himself in the feel of Sean's gentle embrace. They lay there together like that in silence for nearly an hour before they were pulled into the real world once again by the telephone. It was Coleman's phone and it had to be answered. He groaned as if it was painful for him to leave the solace of Sean's supporting touch.

"Hello," he stated as he placed the phone to his ear. Sean could only hear a faint voice coming through the receiver as Coleman listened to what was said.

"Yes." Coleman completed the conversation and then tossed the phone on the bedside table. He pushed his hands through his hair and then turned to look at Sean with a huge smile on his face. "Good morning, Sean. How are you?"

Sean stretched and then sat up. "Good, I'm good."

"You are better than good, so much better than good," Coleman teased him.

Sean blushed but also laughed.

"Would you like to join me in the shower?" Coleman suggested as he stood and began walking toward the bathroom. Sean caught his breath at the sight of Coleman's naked body in all its glory. He was fine, absolutely fine, beyond fine; Sean was tripping over his thoughts as he struggled to form a sentence.

"Thank you, but I have to go." Sean pulled on his boxers and jumped to his feet, then headed toward the adjoining door.

"Wait." Coleman took him by the shoulders and turned him around before he had time to exit the room. He tilted Sean's face up to look at him and slipped his arm around him as he bent to place an affectionate kiss on his lips. "Don't pull away from me, Sean. I don't know about you, but for me that was a mind-blowing evening." He waited for a response. It was a lot for Sean to process, Coleman understood that, but Sean had to feel some of what he was feeling. It was too intense to be his alone.

"Like you said, it was good, even better than good." Sean laughed and returned the kiss, and then, pulling back in order to regard him fully, he said with the smile still on his face, "It's nearly ten and you have an appointment at noon. We need to get moving. If I get in the shower with you...." Sean left it there and waited for understanding, which he got immediately. Coleman agreed and released him.

Sean grabbed the rest of his things and headed for the door. Coleman patted Sean's ass before he left and said, "You are amazing."

"Yes, I know, people tell me that all the time." Sean blew off the compliment.

"I don't doubt that." Coleman was not joking. What Sean didn't know was that this was the first time Coleman had ever called anyone amazing. It wasn't a word that he'd ever used, yet it seemed like the only word that would describe Sean. He watched Sean as he left the room and closed the door behind him. Coleman stood there and stared at the door for several more minutes before finally heading to the shower.

Sean tossed his clothing on his unused bed and pulled his phone out of his pants pocket. He needed to see who had called him so early this morning. Weir had called him. This was puzzling and upsetting. Why would he call him so late or, rather, so early? Why would he call at all? Sean reported once a week like all the interns, and that was the only contact unless problems arose. Sean quickly returned the call, hoping for good news.

"Where were you last night? Why didn't you answer your phone?" Weir barked at him.

"I was asleep. You called at three in the morning," Sean responded carefully.

"Brittany told me that you replaced her on a trip out of town." Weir sounded almost accusatory.

"Mr. West decided to go himself and offered to take me as his assistant for the trip, and I accepted. Why wouldn't I? It is a great opportunity." Sean defended himself without being aggressive.

"You are aware of his reputation?" The professor was still edgy and sharp.

"He's difficult and usually unpleasant to be around," Sean supplied.

"I am referring to his sexual appetite."

Sean cut him off quickly, not wanting to discuss Coleman in these terms. "He is very exclusive, sir, and I find your insinuation insulting."

"I want you back in Chicago by this evening or your internship will be forfeited. Do you understand me?" Weir shouted into the phone. Sean remained silent, seething with indignation at his command. "Do you understand me?

"I understand you," Sean said with all the calm he could pull together.

"Good, I hope you do. I will call you this evening, and f you do not answer, I will take that as your decision to leave the program." Weir was angry, but why?

"Yes, sir." Sean ended the call and sat down on the bed to gather his emotions. He was livid that the professor had the audacity to treat him like a teenager who'd stayed out too late and could not be trusted to take care of himself.

"What was that about?" Sean hadn't realized that Coleman entered the room and had been listening to his conversation Sean turned to see him standing by the opposite side of the bed. He had apparently finished his shower because he was wearing only a towel loosely wrapped around his waist and his hair was wet. Sean struggled with what to say. Say too much and Coleman could get angry enough to do something which could result in him being booted from the program. Weir would not tolerate Sean whining to Coleman about this matter. That would definitely be a deal-breaker.

Say too little and he might not get back to Chicago by this evening, and then he would be booted from the program anyway.

Coleman observed the emotions playing across Sean's face as he tried to figure out what to say and what not to say. He was distressed, that was obvious. Something was weighing heavily upon him and it had something to do with the identity of the caller. "Who were you speaking with?" Coleman thought that might help him ease into an explanation.

"Professor Weir," Sean stated without looking at him.

"He upset you." It was a statement, not a question.

"No, it's nothing, it's fine." Sean tried to sound unaffected but failed. Coleman rounded the bed and pulled him to his feet.

"What did he say to you?" He demanded. Sean tried to avoid eye contact, but Coleman held his chin so he was forced to look up at him.

"He is upset that I replaced Brittany on this trip. He wants me back in Chicago by this evening or my placement will be forfeited." Sean did not want any trouble. He just wanted to complete this placement and get his diploma. He saw Coleman's eyes turn dark and knew that he wanted to say something cutting about Weir. He was holding himself back; Sean could feel the restraint in his hands and his body.

"Do you want me to take care of it?" Coleman asked through clenched teeth.

"No, I don't want to make trouble. Professor Weir is thoughtless and unkind, but he also got me a placement after you tossed my application. He helped me, and I don't want to cause him any trouble." Sean maintained Coleman's gaze in order to make his wishes very clear.

Coleman stared at him for what seemed like forever. His gaze bored into Sean, judging and gauging his next move. He knew that Sean felt a loyalty to Weir, and it ate at him that Weir was using that loyalty to control him. Weir had called him in the middle of the night and then torn into him this morning for not answering. He wanted to separate Sean and Weir. Coleman wanted Weir out of the picture, but for now, he could only do what Sean wanted him to do. He would deal with Weir at a later date. With that promise to himself, he visibly relaxed. "I'll have you back before evening."

Sean smiled and was touched by his understanding of what he needed from him. "Thank you." Sean hurriedly took a shower, dressed, and was ready when Coleman came back into his room to check on his progress.

"The car is ready if you are." He grabbed Sean's backpack and carried it for him as Sean threw his messenger bag over his shoulder.

"What about your bags?" Sean asked offhandedly.

"The porter already took them to the car. You weren't dressed yet, so I didn't send him in here." Coleman smiled and winked at Sean. "I don't want anyone seeing you undressed except me."

Sean laughed, because he thought he was teasing him but he wasn't. Coleman was very serious as far as his possessiveness was concerned. He had never felt like this about anyone in his life; not even as a teenager with his first love had he felt the level of need coupled with jealously that he felt for Sean. He kept waiting for it to subside, to lessen even slightly, but it didn't. The feeling only got larger and more powerful with time.

They completed the meeting with Bail and his accountant and were on their way to the airport by four. The flight was just as rich and elegant on the way back to Chicago. Sean decided he would never get used to this level of comfort and service, but he'd like the opportunity to try. During the flight, Coleman asked him more questions about his relationship with Weir.

"He's my professor, nothing more than that," Sean said.

"He seems to give you a lot of attention; that is why I ask." Coleman was seeing something in Weir's behavior that Sean seemed unable to see. He was acting jealous of Sean's time with Coleman. He was looking at Coleman like a competitor for Sean's attention. Although Weir had helped Sean get a placement, it had not been an altogether altruistic act. He wanted something from Sean, and Coleman was pretty sure what it was.

"He has been good to me, but I don't believe that it is special consideration of any kind. He would do the same for any of his students." Sean gave him his thoughts and was confident that his point of view was the correct one. Weir could look overly concerned, but that was just because he was a good teacher who cared about his students, nothing more. It had really bothered Sean this morning when Weir spoke of Coleman in those derogatory terms, and it was unlike him to be so crass. But still, Sean would not admit that Weir had of late been making him uncomfortable.

"What time is Weir calling you this evening?" Coleman tapped his fingers on the table in front of him and studied Sean through eyes that seemed to be consuming him.

"He said this evening; he didn't give me a time."

"So you have to sit with your phone all evening, waiting for him to decide to call you."

"Yes."

"And this is all because you replaced Brittany and accompanied me to Cleveland for an overnight stay." Coleman continued to tap and stare.

"Yes." Sean was beginning to feel like he was being interrogated.

Coleman didn't pursue the questions any further. He knew the answers already; he was just trying to get Sean to see the truth. He wanted to get Sean thinking about Weir and questioning him and his motives. Coleman dropped Sean at his apartment at 6:00 p.m. He kissed him on the lips and told him good night.

NINE

SEAN thought about their discussion for the rest of the evening. Weir called at six forty-five, which seemed a little early to Sean, but he was just glad Coleman had gotten him home on time. Sean had to admit Coleman was very good at reading people. He knew Weir would call early in hopes of catching him not there and then he would call later and tear into him. But that didn't happen. Sean could hear the disappointment in Weir's voice as he discussed the inappropriateness of Sean taking Brittany's position on the trip. He refused to listen to the fact that Sean had no power over that decision, and instead, wanted to place blame and foster guilt. Thanks to Coleman and his prep work on the plane, Sean smiled to himself as he listened to Weir drone on and on.

Weir finished with, "If you ever leave the city with him again, you call me first and get permission, understood?"

"Yes, sir, I understand." Sean really didn't, but he didn't want to engage him with questions. He just wanted to hang up.

Tim Weir could hear in his voice that he had disengaged. He was probably nodding appropriately, but he wasn't listening anymore. He was worried about Sean. He was an impressionable, kind, easygoing, small-town sort of individual who could easily be taken advantage of, especially by someone like Coleman. Weir had called early because he was hoping West hadn't brought him back yet and it would give him an excuse to remove Sean from the placement. He wanted him out of there and away from West. He'd spent the past two years getting close to Sean, nurturing their relationship, waiting for him to graduate so he could make his next move, and then Coleman came on the scene and just took what he wanted.

"Don't fall for his tender manipulations, Sean. He is a man who gets what he wants and then will toss you aside. Don't be one of his conquests." Weir decided it was time to infuse him with a little healthy fear and doubt. "He is thirty-two years old and has never had a serious relationship, not even one. He hasn't even maintained a relationship for longer than two weeks. The reason I know that is because he boasts of that fact." He fell silent, waiting for a response.

"Yes, sir," was all Sean could say to that little piece of information. He added after a moment of thought, "I'm not a child, Professor. I can take care of myself." After the call ended, Sean went to the kitchen and made himself a cup of tea, then sat down in the living room with the intention of watching television, but instead just stared out the window at the horizon for about twenty minutes. The professor had planted a seed, a hateful seed of insecurity, and it took root as he sat and thought and stared out the window. Would he be the talk of the eighth floor tomorrow? Would Coleman discuss him like one would a prom date who gave it up with little coaxing, while laughing and patting himself on the back? It was his own doing, he finally declared to himself. Coleman hadn't done anything Sean did not want. It wasn't Coleman's fault that Sean couldn't say no. Sean took full responsibility for himself and his own actions and then, suddenly, he felt back in control. *I took as much as I gave,* he declared with a smile. *If it ends here, then so be it.* He raised his cup to the setting sun and shouted, "I had a good time."

COLEMAN drove all the way out to the country estate. He wanted to relax and make some calls, and he did not want to be disturbed. If Sean needed him, he had his cell number and could reach him on that. Coleman wouldn't answer the phone for anyone but Sean. He doubted Sean would call; he had an independent streak that ran deep. He probably wouldn't call anyone unless it was a matter of life or death.

Coleman began his investigation by calling Ed. "Ed, I wanted to ask you a few questions about Tim Weir," He found out that Weir had had several relationships over the years with departing students. It always looked perfectly respectable because they were no longer in school when he completed his pursuit. Ed was very careful about what he shared, but it was clear to Coleman that it was not an aspect of Weir's character that Ed condoned. Coleman then called one of the members of the board of regents and discussed Weir's standing at the university. He discovered there had been at least one complaint against him for stalking, but it was dropped before any legal action took place and therefore had not affected his position at the university.

Coleman paced, considering his options and knowing he could do nothing. Sean would be offended; he had a set of rules he lived by, and Coleman knew he would have to respect those rules. He had to move cautiously, but in the end he promised himself he would deal with the professor.

Sean was just getting ready for bed when the phone rang. He hoped it wasn't Weir again. He'd had all of that man he could stomach for one day. He answered it and said, "Hello."

"I just wanted to say good night and tell you what a wonderful companion you are," Coleman said in such a sexy tone of voice that Sean was instantly hot.

"Thank you, you're not so bad yourself," Sean replied, but he was unable to achieve the same intonation. It was very clear to Sean that Coleman was adept at the art of seduction and Sean was enjoying every minute of it, for as long as it lasted. The last thought spoiled the experience a bit, and Sean found himself abruptly pulled back to reality.

"How did your call go?" Coleman got to the point. He'd tried to resist calling and asking but failed. Weir was turning into an irritant, and Coleman wanted to keep track of him and his activities.

"He called early, which surprised me," Sean began. "He called at a quarter to seven. I appreciate you getting me back here." Sean paused.

"I thought he would call fairly early," Coleman supplied.

"He asked me not to go on any out-of-town trips without clearing it with him first," Sean said and let it lie there for a few moments.

"He said more than that," Coleman prompted. "I won't be offended—please go ahead and tell me." His tone was so smooth, so coaxing, that Sean spilled nearly the entire conversation.

"He thinks I might be taken advantage of, and he is trying to protect me, I suppose. I told him I was well able to care for myself, but I have to do as he says as far as my placement here. He holds all the cards, and he could have me removed at any time." Sean felt like he was babbling but didn't want to get Coleman upset or get the professor in trouble.

"I understand. You are in a tough spot, and I will not make it more difficult for you if I can help it." Coleman struggled to remain thoughtful and considerate while the impudence of Weir was burning a hole through him.

"I'm sorry for Weir's behavior," Sean offered.

"You have nothing to be sorry for except perhaps a case of misplaced loyalty." Coleman was doing his best but had to throw out at least one negative comment.

"Yes, you're probably correct, but right now he has me over a barrel." Sean used the phrase without thinking it through.

"No one but me will ever have the pleasure of having you over a barrel; that sounds rather kinky," he said and laughed when he heard Sean's indignant gasp. Coleman changed the subject. "I'm going to be away for a few days. I have business up north, but I will be back on Friday. I would like to take you out for dinner Friday night, say, seven o'clock." Coleman was going north to do more research on Weir and on Sean. He found that he cared more than was his usual for the young man, and he wanted, no, *needed* to know all there was to know about him. As far as Weir was concerned, Coleman was simply gathering ammunition for a later battle.

"I would like that. Thank you for the invitation." Sean was again so formal.

"It isn't an invitation, it is a date. I'm asking you out on a date," Coleman clarified good-naturedly.

"Oh, then yes," Sean corrected.

They talked on for a while longer about a variety of subjects, from the professional to the mundane. Coleman was amazed anew at how much he enjoyed just talking with Sean. It was well past midnight when they finally hung up.

At work the next day, Sean was immediately cornered in the lobby by Brittany. She looked very smug and snidely asked, "So, did you get a call from Weir by any chance during your little getaway with the boss?"

Sean looked down his nose at her and said very clearly, "You might want to be a little more careful when trying to assuage your wounded ego at my expense. The boss, as you call him, was not impressed, and he is not stupid either. He is very aware of who would have had reason to contact Weir, and he will probably deal with you when he returns." Sean had no idea if Coleman had a clue as to Brittany's involvement, but he wanted her to be scared; he wanted her to stop being such a total bitch. He watched as the smug grin fell from her face and was replaced with sheer horror. She turned and ran from him and got onto the elevator. Sean watched her go and wondered if he'd been too mean but decided no, she was a bitch, and there was nothing wrong with a little healthy retribution. He smiled to himself and made his way to the third floor.

"Did it go well?" Ed asked as Sean entered the office.

Sean felt bad because his discussion with Brittany had held him up and he hadn't arrived early enough to fix Ed's coffee. "It was an experience," he said and sat down in one of the office chairs. "Mr. West is really interesting to watch when dealing with a client. I learned some great interview techniques."

"Did he treat you okay? Was he respectful of you? He can be unpleasant with people. I've seen him take apart an intern for the smallest infraction. I would really hate for him to do that to you." Ed still worried that Coleman would do something unkind to Sean. The man had it in him to be mean… very mean. "I'm glad he was decent with you."

The rest of the day was uneventful. Sean found himself thinking about Coleman almost every hour on the hour, and he would push it away and try to focus on whatever project he was involved with. He wished he had a better grasp on what was happening between them and what Coleman expected of him. When he thought about it too much, he began to get spooked. Coleman was way out of his league and able to do better, much better. Why was he with Sean? What was his motivation? Was it purely physical? Or did he really want to be friends? It seemed unlikely someone like Coleman would want to be friends with someone like him.

He decided to let it go because the more he thought about it, the more caught up in Coleman he became. He had to take it as it came and not expect anything, or he was going to be in for a big letdown. Coleman was a player: he did not have relationships, and he did not stay with one person longer than a week or two. Sean needed to stay grounded in reality and not let himself get trapped in the fantasy that was Coleman West. "Enjoy it while it lasts," he said to himself. He thought he might get a T-shirt with that phrase printed on it in order to help him with the grounding part.

COLEMAN met with one of the regents and took him to lunch. They discussed possible donations, and the honors associated with a donation, and then Coleman steered the conversation in the direction of Weir. He learned not only did Weir have a stalking charge that was later dropped, but he'd also been accused of sexual harassment by one of his male secretaries. He had been required to take sensitivity training and was not reprimanded beyond that. It looked to Coleman like Weir had escaped actual punishment many times, always skating by and getting the minimum.

What surprised him the most was that the regent told Coleman that Weir was currently in a committed relationship with a man who worked as a library technician. It looked like Weir was preparing to trade the library technician in for a legal assistant. He needed to get Sean away from this man, away from his influence and control. Coleman planned on presenting his findings to Sean when he returned and hoped Sean would give him the go-ahead to destroy Weir.

That last thought made him pause. Never had he waited for someone to give him permission; never did he wait when every part of him wanted retribution. Sean was having a big effect on him. Coleman laughed because he knew he would do nothing to Weir until Sean said it was okay. What a bizarre feeling, he thought, to have someone else's needs take precedence over his own. He spoke to the owner of the pub where Sean had worked, and to his neighbors, who all described Sean as the finest individual they have ever known. The praise and support they dished out made Coleman feel like he had found a saint. He smiled, beamed almost, as they told him how honest Sean was, how hardworking, helpful, reliable, kind, and that he'd been the most dutiful son ever put on the earth. They didn't tell him anything he didn't already know.

ON THURSDAY morning, Sean was on his way to work and looking forward to seeing Coleman the next day. He missed Coleman's presence, his comments. He missed him and he admitted it to himself. Coleman was having a powerful effect on him, and he knew it probably wasn't healthy, but he would be returning to Mt. Pleasant in a few weeks and by then it would all be over for certain, anyway. "Enjoy it while it lasts," he mumbled to himself and then he added, "I really need to get that T-shirt made."

After lunch, which he packed himself and ate at his desk, he went to the third-floor restroom to wash up. It was empty, and he was just drying his hands when a large man who looked to be in his late twenties entered and asked him if his name was Sean Robbins.

"Yes," Sean said tentatively, slightly taken aback at being approached like this in a washroom. The man looked menacing. Sean stepped back from him as the man continued to advance. Suddenly, he lunged at Sean, grabbed him around the throat and slammed him up against the wall. The man had his face right up next to his when he spoke. Sean pulled at the hand around his throat but couldn't remove it.

"This is from Brittany, you little prick," the man whispered through clenched teeth, spraying Sean's face with spittle as he did so. Then he punched him in the stomach and swung his fist twice more, connecting with the side of Sean's face. The impact of the last punch brought Sean down to the floor in a crumpled heap.

Sean lay on the washroom floor, barely conscious. Through a haze, he heard the man say, "Brittany sends her love."

Sean came to slowly. Thankfully, the bathroom remained empty. With great effort and will, he managed to pull himself to his feet and look in the mirror. He was in rough shape and there was blood everywhere. He needed help but he didn't want to make a scene at work. He took the cell phone Coleman had given him out of his pocket and called Ed, who would know how to handle th s; he would help him.

"Hello, Mr. Murray," he mumbled between rapidly sw₂lling lips. He paused to spit blood into the sink.

"Sean, what's wrong?" Ed came to his feet and started walking into the hallway. Sean had just been at his desk; where was he? "Where are you?"

"Would you come to the washroom on this floor? I neec your help." All Sean heard was a click as Ed hung up, and within seconds, he was rushing into the washroom. Sean turned to lcok at him and heard him gasp.

"What the hell happened?" Ed went to him and put his arm around him for support.

Sean just shook his head. "I need to get out of here without making a scene. I don't want everyone to know I took a beat_ng in the bathroom. Can you get me out of here?" he pleaded. He didn't want to be the gossip of the day or the week; he just wanted to go home and pull himself together.

"I should call the police," Ed insisted.

"No, just leave it. It was Brittany Saunders's brother, Adam." Sean had recognized him after the man had mentioned Britany's name.

"Why would he do such a thing?" Ed took a few paper towels, wet them, and began cleaning Sean up very carefully.

"Brittany and I have been adversaries for quite some time." Sean's face stung on contact with the towel. "Ouch."

"Sorry, I'll be more careful."

"It's okay. I appreciate your help, thank you so much."

"You were explaining, you and Brittany don't get along." Ed prompted him to continue while he wet some more towels and began to clean the sink and floor.

"She really gets upset... and... she thinks that I am usurping her position here with Mr. West, and she is... really mad." Sean was having difficulty keeping focused. His head was aching and his vision was fading. "She's never had her brother beat me up before."

"Sean, let me call the police," Ed demanded.

"I can't take the embarrassment—please don't." Sean leaned on the sink, pressed a cold towel to his eye, and winced at the pain that shot through his face. "It's Thursday. If I can get home, I can stay home tomorrow, and I should be looking sort of okay by Monday. No one needs to know this happened here."

"What if he comes after you again?" Ed completed wiping up the floor and tossed the towels in the trash.

"I'll be more careful. It won't happen again." Sean looked at him with his one good eye and implored him to understand.

"It goes against my better judgment, but okay. I'll let you make the call this time. I'm taking you to the hospital, and I will not take no for an answer." Ed put his arm around him, and they started walking toward the door.

"I can make it on my own. I don't want to draw attention to myself." Sean pulled away and walked carefully next to Ed, who was watching him vigilantly and making sure he did not falter. They made it outside and to Ed's car without anyone looking their way or asking questions. Sean was hurting like hell and barely conscious, but he was relieved. No prying eyes and no awkward questions. All he wanted was to go home and lay down.

"I'm taking you to the hospital," Ed announced again.

"Just take me to the clinic. I can't afford the ER," Sean stated.

"I'll pay for it."

"No, please, the clinic. I feel like shit as it is; don't make me feel worse by having you cover the bill." Sean was adamant, so ultimately, Ed gave in and took him to a nearby walk-in clinic.

The medical staff at the clinic determined Sean had a slight concussion. They gave him four stitches in his lip and medicine for his pain. By the time Ed got him to his apartment, Sean's eye had swollen shut and was black and blue, as was the left side of his face. His lip was puffy and red, and he had a hard time talking. Ed helped him out of his jacket, and while removing Sean's tie, he noticed the bruises on his neck.

"He strangled you!" Ed exploded. "Your throat is all bruised. Did the doctor at the clinic see your throat?"

"Yes, it will be fine—no permanent damage," Sean assured him.

"Not for lack of trying. This man could have killed you, Sean. Why are you protecting him?" Ed helped him into his bed and covered him with a blanket.

"I'm not protecting him, I'm protecting myself. I can't cause a scene at the law firm. Mr. West would not look kindly on me bringing the police to the firm." Sean bunched up the pillows under his head and relaxed into them. "I'll be okay in a couple of days. Thank you, Mr. Murray." He closed his one eye and tried to relax.

"Mr. West would not penalize you for calling the police. He would understand," Ed stressed, but Sean didn't respond; he wasn't listening.

Ed put Sean's phone within reach and asked him to please call if he needed anything. Sean assured him he would. Ed also poured Sean a glass of water and set it on the nightstand next to his pain medication. Then he stood there and watched him for a few minutes before leaving the room. The poor kid looked like someone had used him as a punching bag. Sean would probably look even worse tomorrow. Ed wanted to ask him to come home with him, so he and his wife could keep an eye on him, but he knew Sean would refuse the offer. Ed hated leaving him here alone, but after several more minutes of consideration, he let himself out.

Sean's phone began to ring at around seven thirty. He was barely awake and reached very carefully for the phone, which Ed had placed on the bedside table. It hurt to move, and the phone rang several times before Sean could answer it.

"Hello." He spoke out of one side of his mouth.

"Sean, did I wake you?" Coleman was sitting in his hotel room and couldn't get his mind off Sean. For some reason, he felt like Sean needed him. He needed to call and talk to him; he needed to hear his voice.

"Yes, I was just taking a nap." Sean was trying desperately to control the pain that was shooting through his eye. It was excruciating, and he didn't want Coleman to know. As soon as he hung up, he planned on taking one of those pills the doctor had given him.

"Are you okay?" Coleman heard his breathing and the tone of his voice and knew something was not right.

"Yes." Sean didn't elaborate. He slowly swung his legs over the edge of the bed and sat up, wincing slightly as he moved.

"What is it?" Coleman asked again. He could read Sean and he knew something was wrong.

"I'm just not feeling very well." Sean tried to cover. "I'm nauseated and very stiff, maybe the flu."

"Get well, Sean, because we have a date tomorrow." Coleman calmed a little, but he still wasn't completely buying the "not feeling well" statement.

Sean searched his mind for a reason to get out of the date. He couldn't let Coleman see him tomorrow. He would probably look worse than he did right now. What could he tell him? How could he get out of this? "I really don't feel very well. I would rather postpone our date. I doubt I will be feeling much better tomorrow." He left it there. He could hear the intense speculation on the other end of the phone even though Coleman had not said a word.

"I'll call you tomorrow and see how you are feeling," Coleman told him and then added, "good night." He hung up knowing full well Sean was not telling him the whole truth. "Damn it!" he yelled to the empty room and tossed the phone on the bed. He paced the room for a few minutes and then couldn't take it any longer. The only person that Sean trusted implicitly was Ed. If something was wrong with Sean, he would discuss it with Ed. He scrolled through the contacts on his cell phone and found Ed's number.

"Ed, I want to ask you a few questions," Coleman began.

"Yes, sir." Ed had a clue what Coleman wanted to discuss but he was unsure how much he could say, considering it was Sean's information to share, not his.

"I just called Sean, and he sounded strange. What's going on?" He waited.

Ed paused, trying to decide what he could tell him without breaking confidence. He was silent too long, and Coleman broke into his thoughts.

"I know how much Sean trusts and respects you. You are the only person he would talk to if he was in trouble, and that is why I am calling you for answers." Coleman tried to persuade Ed, but felt he wasn't going to get the answers he wanted.

"I can't tell you." Ed struggled with what to say. Coleman deserved to know, but he had promised Sean he would say nothing about it.

Coleman sensed his difficulty. "Is Sean okay? Tell me that much."

"No, he is not okay," Ed stated very clearly, and in an instant, he heard the phone hang up.

That was all Coleman needed to hear. He was on a plane and headed back to Chicago within half an hour. Ed was not someone to overstate a matter. For him to say Sean was not okay was a serious statement. Coleman ran a thousand scenarios over in his mind during the twenty-minute plane ride to Chicago. Most of the scenarios involved Weir. If he had done anything to hurt Sean, Coleman would annihilate him.

Ed drove over to Sean's after speaking with Coleman. He wanted to check on him and make sure he was all right and didn't need to go to the hospital. The clinic was okay, but those bruises on Sean's neck really concerned him. When he got to his apartment,

Sean was just getting out of bed. Ed had taken Sean's keys with him in the event that he needed to get in and Sean was unable to get to the door. Sean looked worse, if that was possible. His face was black and blue and swollen. He could open his right eye a little, but the swelling from the left eye had begun to affect the right. Ed wondered if he would be able to open either eye in the morning.

"Coleman called," Sean said without realizing that he'd used Coleman's first name in front of Mr. Murray. "He asked me to go to dinner with him tomorrow, but I had to try and get out of it. I can't let him see me like this."

"Coleman, is it now?" Ed teased.

"Don't make me laugh, it hurts." Sean chuckled painfully. "He told me he wants to be my friend and gave me permission to use his first name when we are not at the firm. That's all," Sean said, trying to cover.

"He wants to be much more than your friend. Even I can see that, and I'm usually numb to most things that go on around me." He grinned and Sean returned the gesture.

Sean took another pill for the pain and was getting a glass of water to wash it down when his doorbell rang. "Would you get that, Mr. Murray? I really don't want anyone seeing me right now."

Ed opened the door and was shocked to see Coleman standing there with the darkest of expressions on his face. It dared anyone to try and cross him.

"Where is he?" was all he said as he walked into the apartment.

Ed motioned toward the kitchen but did not say a word. Just then, Sean came out of the kitchen and walking into the living room, coming face-to-face with Coleman.

"My God!" was all Coleman could get out upon seeing Sean. His expression changed from darkness to an agonizing shock. He reached out but was afraid to touch him for fear of hurting him. "Sean, Sean," he said and just stared. A darkness laced with rage came over him at that moment "Jesus! What happened to you? Who did this?" The rage that was radiating from him was a most tangible—the two other men could feel it and were being affected by it.

Sean started to breathe heavily, like a man afraid, and Coleman quickly tried to calm him. He reached out to take his hand and hold it. Sean's hand seemed to be the only part of him that wasn't injured. Sean tried to speak, but he was having difficulty due to the swelling of his mouth and the pain in his face. After a few attempts at an explanation, he looked at Ed and nodded permission for him to tell the story.

Coleman listened to Ed but never took his eyes off Sean. He had never considered that Sean had suffered a beating. Who could do this to a person? How could this happen to someone as good and kind as Sean? He planned on finding the person who'd done this and beating the life out of them.

"Who did this to him, Ed?" Coleman's voice was as cold as ice as his eyes took in the bruises and the swelling and the stitches. He noticed the bruising on his throat and lost it. He turned abruptly and grabbed Ed by the shirt collar. "Tell me his name!"

Ed was taken off guard and gasped with shock at the attack. Sean grabbed Coleman's arm and tried to pull him off Mr. Murray.

"Leave him be!" Sean slurred and winced as he opened his mouth too wide and pulled on the stitches. "Shit, that hurts!"

Coleman responded immediately and released Ed, but still held him with a stare.

"Adam Saunders, Brittany's brother," Ed stated very clearly.

Coleman left the apartment without another word, slamming the door behind him. Ed and Sean just stared at each other, wondering what would happen next.

Coleman made a few calls from his car and soon found the whereabouts of Adam Saunders. He was registered at one of the downtown hotels. The rage Coleman felt when he saw Sean and heard what had happened to him was unparalleled to anything he had ever experienced before. He had been angry many times, but rage was something he'd rarely experienced. In the past, he'd never allowed anyone to mean so much to him that mistreatment of them would trigger such a response.

Coleman found Adam and was disgusted with the fact that Adam was at least six feet tall and two hundred pounds. How could any man his size and strength get satisfaction from beating a man the size of Sean? Well, this bully had dished out his last beatdown. Coleman took him down in two punches, one to the stomach and another that caught him under the chin as he was buckling from the first strike. Coleman bent down and explained very clearly, as Adam lay there struggling with consciousness and bleeding, that if he ever went near Sean again, it would be the last thing he ever did.

Adam, frightened and unsure what he had gotten himself into, quickly nodded. He was ready to agree with anything this man said. He had never experienced an attack so sudden and so powerful, and he did not want to push this guy or cause him to come after him again.

"It was very easy for me to find you this time and if you so much as say a coarse word to Sean, I will find you again, and I will finish this, understand?" It took everything Coleman had to hold himself back from beating this man to a pulp. He wanted to crush him for what he'd done to Sean. When the man nodded again, Coleman stood up and abruptly left the room.

Ed and Sean sat together for about an hour before Ed excused himself and again asked Sean to call him if he needed him.

"What do you think he is doing?" Sean threw it out there. He wanted to get Ed's take on the evening's events before he left.

Ed stopped at the door and turned to regard Sean very seriously. "He is finding Adam Saunders and he is dealing with him."

Sean spent the next two hours pacing the floor, waiting and hoping to hear from Coleman. It was twelve thirty in the morning when his doorbell finally rang. Coleman looked as lethal as ever, but there was a satisfaction in his expression that hadn't been there before. Sean noticed that his knuckles were scratched and bruised and assumed he had found and dealt with Adam.

"You're staying with me at my place in the country," he stated as he went to Sean's room and started to pack for him. 'We're stopping at the hospital first, and you're getting a complete physical," he said to him over his shoulder.

Sean stood in the doorway to the bedroom and simply watched as Coleman took complete control of his life. Normally, he would have resisted but he didn't have it in him tonight. Perhaps tomorrow. Sean took his coat and put it on as carefully as possible. Coleman came up behind him and assisted him. Sean hadn't even realized he was there.

"I can see what he did to your face," Coleman began, 'but did he hurt you anywhere else?" His dark eyes were now calm and caring. It touched Sean, and his good eye began to tear up. He let his gaze drop to the floor. It was hard looking at Coleman knowing what he looked like.

"My ribs hurt, he punched me there first—no, actually, he grabbed me by the throat first." He was slowly remembering the attack. "My whole body is aching, but it's just from the shock, I think." Sean took one of his baseball caps and placed it on his head to try and cover the bruises.

Coleman reached out and gently raised Sean's T-shirt in order to get a look at his ribs. He saw the bruising on his ribs and across his stomach.

Sean pulled back, uncomfortable with the exposure. "I'm fine," he stated a little too crisply.

"No, you're not fine, but you will be." Coleman stared at him, trying to figure out what to say. How could he make Sean feel better about this? What could he say that would be even a little helpful? "He won't ever touch you again," he said softly as he took a step closer and slipped his arm around Sean carefully.

"What did you do?" Sean had an idea, considering the marks on his knuckles.

"I took care of it."

Sean knew he wasn't going to get any more explanation than that, so he didn't press for more.

Coleman took him to the hospital, and he went through a battery of tests, all of which determined exactly what the clinic had—he had a slight concussion and should be better in three to four days. Sean was relieved that he didn't have a skull fracture or any internal bleeding; the clinic had not checked for these, and he had been concerned. After the hospital visit, Coleman drove him to his home in the country. It was very early in the morning when they arrived.

Sean assumed he would be in the guest room again, like the last time he'd stayed, but Coleman took his things and brought them to the master bedroom. Sean hung his coat and hat in the closet downstairs and sat down on one of the chairs in the living room. His head was aching something fierce, but he didn't want to take any more painkillers. He'd had enough of those, and it was time to start managing the pain without medication.

Coleman found him in the living room and knelt down in front of his chair with a hand on each of Sean's knees, his touch comforting. "I want you to sleep with me. I want to keep an eye on you and make sure there aren't any complications." He tried to look Sean in the eyes, but Sean dodged his scrutiny and covered his face with one of his hands. Coleman reached up, tenderly pulled the hand away from his face, and brought it down to rest in his lap. "Don't hide from me." He looked at Sean very seriously. "Even bruised and swollen, you're still a fine-looking man and sexy as hell."

"Sure." Sean tried to laugh but the stitches caught him. "Ouch, these stitches are tight."

Coleman reached up and cupped the good side of Sean's face. He needed to touch him and connect with him. He rubbed his thumb over the surface of Sean's upper lip and gently touched the stitches. Very slowly, almost hypnotically, he leaned into him and placed the most tender, exploring kiss on his lips and then proceeded to trail kisses all along his jaw and cheek and both eyes. "So sexy," he mumbled under his breath. "If you weren't in pain, I would have you naked by now."

"Thanks, I needed that." Sean placed his hand on Coleman's shoulder and returned the kiss as well as he could, considering his limitations.

"Come to bed with me, Sean." Coleman helped him to his feet and assisted him into the bedroom. Once there, he helped Sean out of his clothing, leaving him in just his briefs, and helped him into bed. Sean watched with his good eye as Coleman disrobed completely and got into bed with him. Coleman gently pulled Sean to him and had him rest his head on his chest. He placed a loving, protective arm around him, and very soon they were both asleep

TEN

OVER the next couple of days, Sean's bruising got worse and then it got better. By Sunday the bruises were beginning to fade and the swelling was all but gone. He was to go in on Monday and have the stitches removed at the clinic, but Coleman insisted he would have someone come to the house and remove them. Sean was extremely grateful to Coleman for all his help. He hid Sean so no one was aware of what had taken place and took very good care of him. He even had his private doctor come to the house on Saturday to check him out again and make sure everything was okay and nothing had been overlooked. He was a very attentive, somewhat domineering caretaker, but Sean appreciated everything he was doing. With that said, Sean was very anxious to go home. It grated on his independence to have someone doing so much for him. It made him feel like a charity case. He knew that Coleman didn't see him that way, but still, that was how he felt.

Coleman made a very delicious roast beef dinner on Sunday, and afterward asked Sean if he'd like to take a walk. He had constructed a nice nature walk through the woods that sprawled through his property for about two miles. He had some things he wanted to discuss with Sean and wanted no interruptions.

Sean was anxious to get out of the house, and a walk in the woods sounded great. Coleman had kept him either in bed or in a chair for the past couple of days. The guy was definitely a mother hen. Coleman immediately reached down and took his hand, holding it firmly. "I thought maybe I could go home tomorrow," Sean stated casually. "The bruising is under control, and I think I can hide most of what is left. I've taken advantage of you for too long."

Coleman listened but remained silent. His grip tightened, which was Sean's only indication that Coleman had heard him.

"I appreciate everything you have done for me, but I need to let you get back to your life," Sean added.

"You are no trouble, and if anyone is taking advantage, it is me. I have enjoyed your company." Coleman cast his glance down at him as they continued their stroll. "I also understand your need to have your control back. I do think tomorrow may be a bit soon, though. The doctor will be out in the morning to remove your stitches and give you another once-over. Why don't we wait until he gives you a clean bill of health and discuss your moving back home then?"

Sean nodded his agreement. He was sure the doctor would be supportive and would find no reason for him not to return home. He was therefore confident he would be back in his apartment by tomorrow night at the latest, and hopefully be back at work by Tuesday.

"I wanted to discuss a few things with you, Sean," Coleman began as released Sean's hand. He stuck both hands in his pockets and casually continued to walk next to him. Although they were mere inches apart, they weren't touching.

Sean said nothing but turned to look at him, signaling Coleman had his attention. He then turned his gaze back to the tree-lined path in front of them.

"I've looked into your professor's background." Coleman looked at him to see if he was going to react, but Sean kept walking and did not look at him. "He has incidents in his past that include stalking and harassment."

This time, Sean did turn to look at him with a shocked expression, although he didn't comment. They continued walking.

"The victims were one student and one secretary at the university. Complaints were filed in both cases, but no charges. He got off by agreeing to attend sensitivity training in the harassment case, and the stalking was just dropped, no reason given." Coleman stopped talking and waited for Sean to comment on what he'd told him.

"Maybe that was in his past, but he is in a committed relationship now," Sean finally answered.

"The sexual harassment charge was last semester. He is still completing his court-ordered sensitivity training," Coleman countered.

"Why are you telling me this?"

"He has a pattern of going after former students. Weir has had relationships with at least four that I was able to determine. He grooms them by convincing them he has their best interests in mind, he becomes their friend, in some cases, and has used manipulation and guilt to also get what he wants. Once they graduate, he makes his move." Coleman removed his right hand from his pocket and reaching over, took Sean's left hand in his and held it as they walked.

"Do you think he has been grooming me?" Sean still couldn't get his mind around it.

"Yes. I believe he plans on making his move at the end of the summer. You don't owe him anything; he does a job that he gets paid for. If you owe anyone it is Ed Murray and no one else—remember that." Coleman punctuated his statement with a squeeze of Sean's hand.

"He has control over this internship, so I have to do as he says to a certain extent—as far as it relates to this placement, anyway," Sean explained, but he knew if Weir did anything out of line or the least bit suggestive of the outcome Coleman expected, he would leave the placement rather than comply.

"He has no real control over you except that which you give him. If you want him gone, I will make that happen. If you want someone else to oversee your internship, I will make that happen. Tell me what you want, and I will give it to you," Coleman said softly but with intensity. He wanted Sean away from Weir but couldn't do anything without his permission. If he did, Sean would see it as trading one controller for another. It was his life and therefore his call.

"Thank you for the offer, but I have to handle this myself." Sean contemplated what Coleman had said and would have liked to take him up on the change of supervisor, but he had to do this himself. He couldn't be seen as so weak that someone else had to take care of him. No, that would look really bad.

"Okay, but if he hurts you, I will hurt him right back. On that you have my promise. I won't wait for your permission; I will just deal with him."

"You can't keep fighting my battles." Sean was firm on that point.

"I protect what's mine. That's who I am, so get used to it, Sean."

The statement was spoken casually, yet it hit Sean like an electric shock. He was flattered and appalled at the same time. He decided to let it pass without comment. What could he say? By referring to him as his, did Coleman mean he thought he owned him? Did he look upon Sean the way he looked at his watch or car? The more Sean thought about it, the more unsettled he became. Was it really Weir who was doing the grooming? After their night together in Cleveland, he had begun to believe perhaps Coleman would make a place for him in his life, but maybe he'd been deceiving himself. Coleman had said so himself—he had never had a relationship and had never included anyone in his life. He had been nothing but honest with Sean. As much as Sean ached to believe otherwise, his time with Coleman would end, probably sooner than later. He'd already had a longer run than most. In a few weeks, his internship would come to an end and he would return to Mt. Pleasant. Their union would end then, unless Coleman tired of him sooner. Whatever the timetable on his exit from Coleman's life, Sean wanted to enjoy the time that he had with him now. *I knew the score when I started this relationship, so I have no right to get upset or expect more*, he told himself once again.

"You look very pensive, Sean," Coleman commented with a grin. "What are you thinking about that has you so serious?"

"Oh, just life in general," Sean said. It wasn't a lie, just not entire truth. Thankfully, Coleman didn't press for more.

After walking for a while longer, they made their way back to the house. They sat together in the living room with tea and were watching the History Channel when Coleman could take it no longer.

"Okay, Sean, ever since our walk this afternoon, you have been a million miles away from me. What's up?"

Sean was caught up in his own considerations when Coleman made the statement and was abruptly pulled back to the man sitting beside him. "I'm fine, what do you mean?" He didn't look at him. Coleman riveted him with a stare and prolonged silence that caused Sean to finally look at him. The intensity was such that Sean was drawn to him and could not stay disconnected.

Coleman gently encircled Sean's mid-section and pulled him into his lap so that he was lying on his back across Coleman's thighs with his head held in the palm of Coleman's hand. Coleman bent his head slowly, taking in Sean's trepidation-filled eyes and his full, red lips, which parted as he moved closer still. Coleman could see that Sean wanted him but was uncertain. Coleman wanted to smile and be playful in an attempt to pull him out of his heavy thoughts, but the look on Sean's face, the desire, the need went right to his groin and exploded there. Nothing was going to prevent Coleman from taking him, just as Sean's eyes were begging him to.

"I want you too," he said and then took Sean's mouth in a careful kiss. Coleman explored every contour of Sean's mouth. He'd learned some of Sean's needs back in Cleveland, and one of these, he knew, was kissing. Sean loved to kiss. It pushed his buttons and made him weak, and therefore, as far as Coleman was concerned, kissing was a priority.

Sean lips were still a little sore, but he didn't care. He would endure a little pain in order to have what Coleman was offering. He reached up and threaded his fingers through Coleman's hair, pressing himself closer and drawing all he could from him.

Coleman gripped Sean tightly, forgetting the injuries to his ribs until Sean winced but quickly suppressed the response and moved closer to signal that he was fine. "Don't stop," he breathed into Coleman's mouth.

Coleman gentled his assault as much as was humanly possible for him at that moment. Having Sean so pliable in his arms was exhilarating and stirred him to scoop him up in his arms and carry him to the bedroom. He broke the kiss only when he laid Sean on the bed and began to remove his clothing. They were both naked within minutes, and Coleman stretched out on top of Sean, pressing him into the mattress.

Sean opened up for him and took him in an embrace that was all arms and legs. He wanted Coleman closer, he wanted to consume him, and he tried with his mouth, taking Coleman deeper and wetter. Sean's heart welled with the need to verbalize what he was feeling; he choked back the words that would sink him, the words that would send Coleman running from him. He suppressed the words, and they came out as a groan from the depths of his being.

Coleman registered the depth of Sean's feeling and fell apart. The emotion behind that groan melted his heart and then, just as quickly, exploded in his groin. He grabbed Sean's hips and pushed them to the mattress as he thrust himself against him, over and over, eliciting a gasp and then a moan from Sean that filled the room. Friction, touch, warmth, and fulfillment—Coleman craved them all and he wanted them now.

Sean saw the level of hunger in Coleman's eyes, and it both startled and excited him. Coleman was intent and nothing was going to stop him. Sean ground his pelvis upward in invitation, and Coleman launched. Sean held his breath as Coleman slammed his thighs high and dropped to crush his face into Sean's crotch. He lapped up along his scrotum and devoured him over and over. Sean exhaled a deep growl and grabbed the sheets to anchor himself.

It had been a week since Coleman had tasted Sean, a week since he held him like this, and he felt like a starving man being thrown a steak. He couldn't stop and he had no intention of trying. He moved forward and took Sean's throbbing member in his mouth, causing Sean to squirm and moan his name. Coleman smiled and took him again. He pumped with his mouth and his hand until Sean was nearly breathless and finally called him baby. Oh, he lived for that. "Say it again, Sean. Say it again."

"Baby, you make me tremble. You make me feel so much I think I might burst." It was so hard to speak, yet so gratifying to put words to his emotions. "I need to kiss you."

Coleman responded immediately to the request, capturing Sean's mouth with his own.

COLEMAN lay awake the entire night with Sean in his arms, dreading the daylight, for then Sean would be leaving. Sean wanted to go home; he'd made that very clear. Something had been weighing heavily on him since yesterday, but he wouldn't discuss it. Coleman assumed it had something to do with Weir. Sean was still feeling a misplaced loyalty to the man, and he was probably trying to figure out how to handle the situation. He was the most ethical, loyal, honest individual Coleman had ever met. Sean lived his life by a code that was, Coleman believed, last seen in the days of Camelot. Coleman smiled, brushed the hair back from Sean's eyes, and watched him as he slept.

His plans for Sean stretched long into the future. He knew that now as well as he knew his own name. Coleman would not let him go. As much as he'd never wanted a relationship, never wanted a binding connection, he wanted Sean and he accepted the fact that he would not have a truly happy life without him. If he could persuade Sean to love him and declare that love, Sean would never leave him, unless he asked him to leave, which was something he would never do. The men in his past had never touched him beyond the physical, and he'd had no qualms about asking them to leave. Sean had managed to touch him in every possible way before they became physical, which totally sealed the deal for Coleman. He was completely taken the first time Sean stared into his eyes and touched him intimately. Sean's hand was soft and gentle, but also strong and determined as he remembered his own shudders and gasps from the night before. Coleman smiled again and raised his hand to touch Sean's face, running his fingers along his jaw and over his lips. He'd learned that first time in Cleveland that sex was much more intense and powerful and passionate when you were with someone you loved. He would have to tell Sean how he felt very soon; put it out there and see if he reciprocated.

"Good morning, Sean," Coleman said as Sean stretched and settled back down with their faces inches apart.

"Good morning," Sean groaned but also smiled. He raised his hand and cupped Coleman's cheek, rubbing his thumb lightly over his bottom lip.

Coleman let this go on for about a minute before he captured Sean's thumb in his mouth and sucked on it mercilessly. Then he rolled on top of him and continued his ministrations with his mouth and his hands.

After a shower, Coleman helped Sean dry himself off. He found he had a tough time keeping his hands off Sean and drying him seemed a good excuse to continue touching him. Once finished,

Coleman came up behind him and wrapped his arms around him. He squeezed Sean close and pressed his lips to his ear, whispering, "You're a very sexy man, Sean Robbins."

Sean leaned back into him, marveling at the strength and comfort that Coleman gave him. He closed his eyes and tried to commit it all to memory for those long, lonely nights awaiting him in Mt. Pleasant.

They finished dressing and Coleman prepared breakfast. Sean offered to help, but Coleman told him again, like every other morning, to sit and relax. He enjoyed fussing in the kitchen and he enjoyed feeding Sean, who was always so grateful and complimentary of anything Coleman did for him that Coleman had begun to thrive on the praise. He handed Sean his plate and planted a wet kiss on his lips as he did so. Sean smiled, accepted the breakfast, and as usual, raved about its taste and presentation.

"I'm going to have to have you over soon, so I can reciprocate," Sean said as he ate the scrambled eggs, ham, and toast, and drank his fresh coffee.

"How about next Sunday morning?"

"It's a date," Sean exclaimed. Then he added, "Why don't you stay Saturday night and then I'll serve you breakfast for a change."

Coleman raised his eyebrows and then winked at him. "Now that is definitely a date." He took a sip of coffee and then asked, "Is your shower big enough for the two of us?"

Sean started to laugh and Coleman joined. "Yes, it is, and it has a little bench too."

"Could be interesting." Coleman refilled Sean's coffee cup and then they moved out onto the patio for the fresh air.

"When is the doctor coming?" Sean asked.

"Before noon," Coleman answered and then added, "You're welcome to stay here as long as you like. Don't feel that you have to go home."

"I have to get back to my internship, and I don't want to keep you away from work any longer," Sean reasoned, although he would have loved to stay longer. That part of him—the romantic, unrealistic part—wanted to stay and pretend they were a real couple. Here at Coleman's country estate, it felt real; it felt like they were in an honest relationship. But back home, questions bombarded him and uncertainty engulfed him.

"Don't use me as an excuse; you're not keeping me from anything," Coleman responded and turned to look Sean in the eye.

Sean smiled and took his hand. "Thank you, but if I don't get back to work soon, people are going to start talking."

"Let them talk," Coleman declared.

"Easy for you to say. They might call you the opportunist, but I will be labeled the gold digger, or they'll say that I got to the top by lying on my back and probably many other colorful analogies." Sean shook his head in disgust.

Coleman rubbed his chin and then very thoughtfully announced, "Hmm... lying on your back... that's not our usual. Mostly, I'm on my back with you all over me like a little rhesus monkey." He could barely control his laughter as he watched Sean very calmly set his tea on the table and then turn to look at him with a deadly expression.

Sean didn't say a word but suddenly jumped him and tried to bring him to the ground. Coleman stumbled out onto the lawn with Sean wrapped around him before allowing Sean to take him down. Coleman was shaking and out of breath, he was laughing so hard. Effortlessly, Coleman rolled and pinned Sean to the ground as he continued to try and fight back. Finally, Sean too was out of breath and stopped his resistance.

Coleman lay on top of him, pinning Sean's hands to the ground above his head. "Do you give up?" He continued to chuckle at Sean's expression of tired exasperation.

"Never. I'm just taking a breather." Sean shifted several times under him and finally Coleman could take no more.

"If you keep up the grinding, I will not be responsible for my actions." The laughter subsided and a heavy sexual tension rose between them. Coleman released one of Sean's hands in order to free his own to roam Sean's face. Coleman lightly brushed Sean's hair back from his forehead and then wandered lower, to his lips, where he gently pulled on his bottom lip until Sean opened his mouth. Once this had been achieved, Coleman quickly slipped his hand behind Sean's neck, pulled him to him, and took his mouth in a tantalizingly sweet kiss. He touched and tasted and probed for a very long time, and Sean enjoyed every minute. He felt valued, important—cherished, even. It was incredible. Coleman was a master of seduction. This last thought sent a chill through Sean that Coleman sensed.

Coleman pulled back and looked Sean in the eyes, trying to read the emotion he'd just felt. "What is it?" he asked while simultaneously gripping him tighter.

"The doctor should be here soon." It was the only explanation Sean could come up with. He wasn't about to explain what he was really thinking. *I was just thinking about how adept you are at getting what you want and getting rid of it when you are finished.* No, that would not be wise to discuss at the moment. Sean wished he hadn't allowed himself to get so caught up in Coleman. When it ended, which it would, he was going to hurt for a long time, and that was a fact.

"Hey, where are you?" Coleman pulled at Sean's hand, cajoling him back from his thoughts.

Sean smiled but his eyes remained troubled.

Coleman continued to playfully nip at his lip and cover his face with light kisses until they noticed a car driving up through the woods. It had to be the doctor, they both surmised, and so they got up and made themselves presentable before he arrived. Coleman brushed off the back of Sean's pants and shirt and then ran his hand through Sean's hair, setting it right and smiling. He seemed to fall into the role of caretaker very easily and comfortably. He then took Sean's hand and led him back into the house.

The doctor removed Sean's stitches and checked all of the bruising, then declared he was doing well, and was almost completely healed. During the entire checkup, Coleman remained at his side, taking in everything the doctor said and constantly questioning, to the point that Sean was becoming annoyed. The doctor noticed and took Coleman out to the other room to talk and let Sean get dressed. Sean could tell that Coleman and the doctor were friends or at least knew each other quite well.

"He is fine, Coleman," the doctor insisted with a pat on his shoulder. "The bruising is nearly all gone, and the tests show no internal damage. He is fine," he repeated.

Coleman stared at him intently, gauging for himself the truth of his statements. "What about possible complications?"

"If there were going to be any, they would have presented themselves by now."

At that moment Sean came out into the main room and asked the doctor if he was well enough to go home and go back to work. The doctor, after a quick glance at Coleman, told him he could absolutely go back to life as normal

Sean returned home that evening. Coleman loaned him one of his cars because he wanted to stay at the estate a couple more days to complete a project he was working on with Jason. It took quite a bit of convincing to get Sean to take the car, but in the end Coleman made it clear that he had two choices: either Sean took the car, or Coleman would drive him home and then return to the estate. Calling a cab was out of the question. Not wanting to put Coleman out any more than he already had, Sean accepted the car.

Jason arrived at the estate just before seven. He had been to Coleman's country home only twice in the past, and was pleased to have been given another invitation. He assumed it was because Coleman didn't want to leave Sean and come back to town, but whatever the reason, Jason was glad to see Coleman. Ever since he got involved with Sean Robbins, he'd had very little time for his old friend Jason. They hadn't been out since Minneapolis, and that hadn't amounted to much either. Coleman wouldn't let himself go and enjoy because he couldn't get his mind off that young man. Jason thought he might have preferred his friend to be ruthless, cold, and unattached. That was the man he knew. Jason didn't remember Coleman ever allowing himself to get this close to someone. He made sure his men knew the score before starting an affair. Coleman was not interested in a relationship and he was not interested in anything even remotely long-term. Most of the men Coleman dated knew and accepted this, so they didn't get hurt when the affair came to an end. There were a couple who had fancied themselves more important than they actually were and they'd been devastated by his ultimate rebuff.

Coleman led Jason into the study where they sat and discussed the Buckland merger, which was to wrap up later in the week. Jason managed to turn the business meeting into a discussion of Sean after about two hours.

"Where is Sean?" He thought he asked casually, but Coleman raised his eyebrows and caught him in a steely gaze.

"Home, I assume. Why do you ask?"

"I heard he spent the weekend here with you." Jason took the file he had on his lap, set it on the desk, and took another.

"Who told you that?" Coleman demanded. His gaze had not lost its intensity and did not waver from Jason's face.

"It's hardly a secret that you're seeing him." Jason tried to clarify his statement. "I don't think it's a particularly good idea to be getting so involved with a university intern, but then it is none of my business."

'You're right; it is none of your business." Coleman was blunt and refused to discuss the matter any further.

Jason left well after one in the morning. They did not discuss Sean again after Coleman made it clear the subject was off-limits. Jason let it go for now, but Coleman's relationship with that young man concerned him more than just a little. He'd heard about the beatdown the kid had taken in the washroom, and how later on, the perpetrator had suddenly found himself all bruised and bleeding, lying on the floor of his own hotel room. It didn't take a genius to know who put the beatdown on the bully. Coleman was not above violence when it came to matters of retribution. He obviously cared for the kid. A part of him wanted to warn Sean, let him know the kind of man, lover, whatever, Coleman was and to please no take anything too seriously, but he didn't know the kid well enough and chances were he wouldn't believe him anyway. He guessed Sean had had more than his share of pain and disappointments in his young life, and unfortunately, Jason believed he had more painful disappointments to come. When Coleman was finished with someone, he was finished in every sense of the word. Jason wondered if Sean would be able to overcome the Coleman West level of rejection. Sean was strong and capable, but emotional pain could bring down some of the toughest, meanest men around. Jason didn't hold out much hope for Sean, if he was truly buying what Coleman was selling.

ELEVEN

THE next few days went by quickly for Sean. Ed kept him busy with research and court and filled his evenings with more research, but Sean didn't mind because it kept his mind off Coleman. He hadn't heard from Coleman since Monday night, but that wasn't unusual when he was caught up in a case, as his time was at a premium.

It was now Thursday night, and Sean had finished dinner and was sitting in front of the television looking for anything that looked the least bit interesting. He was surfing the channels for the fourth time when his doorbell rang. Certain that it was Coleman, Sean hurried to the door expectantly. He'd missed him these past few days and longed to hold and be held, longed to hear his words of encouragement and support, and longed to feel his hands and his lips upon him. When he opened the door, he was startled to see Jason standing there. Sean simply stared at him for a moment before inviting him inside.

"Can we talk?" Jason asked in a soft tone. His expression was one of compassion, and therefore, Sean was instantly filled with dread.

"Sure." Sean led him into the living room and they sat down together. Jason leaned forward in his chair, resting his forearms on his thighs and pinning Sean with a thoughtful gaze.

"I realize you don't know me very well, but I feel know you." Jason paused to register Sean's response, but none came. Sean sat silent and waiting with his gaze cast to the floor. "Coleman has talked about you a lot, and he seems very impressed and taken with you. The reason I am here is because you are not like any man he has had in the past. You are...." This was proving more difficult than he had imagined. How did you warn someone that the person they were in love with was using them for sport? "You are a good man, Sean. You don't deserve what Coleman will most likely do to you."

That statement had Sean raising his gaze to lock with Jason's, but he still did not speak.

"Coleman is a very hard man; he isn't evil, but he isn't kind and he takes care of only himself. He will never allow anyone to get too close, and he will never allow a man to become too important. He learned well from his parents and has vowed never to enter into any relationships. There is no future for you with Coleman. I see you as so much more than any of the other men he has been with, and I want you to know and to understand that he will abandon you." Jason's voice became firm and clear as he finished his statement. "He will leave you and it will not be pleasant. The best you can hope for is that he simply decides to ignore you. I have witnessed him humiliate and destroy men who tried to push or demand anything from him other than the emotional scraps he was providing. Don't be one of those men, Sean. He will eat you alive, and I doubt very much if you could survive such an attack."

Sean finally spoke. "I thought he was your friend?"

"He is, and he is a good friend, but I would never want to be his boyfriend." Jason hoped Sean understood and would protect himself.

"Thank you," was all Sean said.

That night, Sean lay awake, thinking and reviewing every word Jason had said. He had been Coleman's closest friend for over ten years, so he had to know what he was saying. He feared for Sean enough to come and warn him not to get too involved, and that was very chilling. Sean admitted to himself that he was in love with Coleman. It was a feeling that would never be reciprocated, but he loved him anyway. He would have to get ahold of himself and get prepared for the inevitable breakup. The thought brought with it an all-encompassing sadness that stayed until the sun showed through his window. He had been careful and had known before Jason explained it in painful clarity that there was no future. Sean had known this from the beginning and still he had managed to lose his heart.

Another two days passed, and still Coleman had not contacted him. Perhaps the end had already come and Sean just hadn't realized it, Sean thought as he grabbed his coat and headed out for a walk around the area. There had been enough moping around the apartment. It was time to get out. He had a quick burger at an outdoor vendor and then sat in the park for a while before heading back to the apartment. It was nearly eight, and a part of him that hoped Coleman would give him a call, even if it was to tell him he wouldn't be calling anymore. He needed to *know* that it was over, not just figure it out.

As he turned the corner, his attention was caught by a familiar tall, dark man. It was Coleman, and there was another man with him. Coleman was escorting him into a restaurant. He had his hand on the man's shoulder, and he appeared to be very happy. Sean stood as if made of stone and just stared. He couldn't pull his eyes away until they disappeared together into the building. His heart fell to the sidewalk and his breathing became shallow and labored. Sean was shocked by his own reaction to the scene he had just witnessed. He actually thought he might throw up. Sean went to his apartment as quickly as he could, considering he was about a mile away. He needed to get someplace where he could collapse and think and fall apart. It had never occurred to him that he would feel this flat, this empty, this destroyed by Coleman's rejection. Sean was well into angry self-reproach by the time he unlocked his apartment and threw his jacket across the room. "Damn it, I should have known better. What the hell is wrong with me?" he said to the empty room. Sean stalked back and forth across the room and continued to rant at himself about his stupidity.

It was a very rough night and day, but by Sunday he had come to terms with what had happened. He recalled a phrase his mother often quoted to him when he was upset, which was, "Walk in wisdom, not emotion." He repeated this over and over until he started to feel it and then started to live it, and then his mind calmed and acceptance began.

Sean rose early Sunday morning and dressed in a sweatshirt and jeans. He was prepared to meet the day and was determined to enjoy it. Coleman had promised to have breakfast with him this morning, but Sean was quite sure that was not going to happen. Coleman and his new man were doubtless relaxing at his country estate. He was probably making him a nice breakfast and discussing their mutual affection. "Shut up!" he yelled at the direction of his thoughts. "Quit, just quit—it's over."

He scanned the newspaper as he drank his morning coffee and ate a piece of cinnamon toast. He was going to do something this evening and he hoped to find some ideas in the lifestyle section. He perked up when he saw a gallery exhibition open to the public. Just what he needed—some public art and culture. He decided to call Ed and see if he would go with him to the gallery. He scrolled through his contacts and found Ed's number.

"Mr. Murray, sorry to call you so early but I was wondering if you were doing anything this evening, and if not if you would consider going with me to the gallery exhibit at the Morgan?" Sean got it all out in one breath.

Ed laughed. "Mary is at her mother's for the weekend, so as a matter of fact, I am quite free this evening and would love to go with you to the Morgan." He continued to chuckle. "Is this a date, Sean?"

"Would that make you uncomfortable?" Sean teased.

"Not at all, I'm an open-minded middle-aged man."

"Well, in that case, yes, it is a date, and I expect you to look comely." Sean was so glad he had called Mr. Murray. He always could make him laugh.

"I'll meet you at your place at seven."

"Sounds good. See you then."

COLEMAN had been working on the merger all week and had been shutting between Chicago and Minneapolis for the past three days, but finally, agreements had been made and the papers were being drawn up. It was a relief, and a financial and PR boon for the firm. He looked forward to seeing Sean. He would be home this afternoon and would call him as soon as he arrived. Now that he was free to think about something other than work, he began to think about Sean and anxiety hit him. He hadn't spoken with him since Sean left the estate on Monday and that was almost a week ago. He soon realized that he had been so wrapped up in the merger that he had missed the date they had set up. He should have called Sean, should have made the time. What had he been thinking? A subtle panic consumed Coleman, and he immediately grabbed his phone.

Sean was sitting in the park sketching people when his phone rang. He checked the ID and his breath caught in his throat. Why would Coleman be calling now? He didn't need to hear anything from him now. He'd seen enough to know that it was over.

"Hello?" Sean said cautiously.

"Hello, Sean. Have you missed me? I've missed you." Coleman spoke with a confidence he was not feeling.

Sean was not sure what to say or what Coleman was really asking. *It's over. He has someone else. Why would he want me to miss him?*

He was quiet too long, so Coleman filled the silence. "May I see you tonight? May I take you to dinner?" Coleman felt the distance growing between them and it tore at his heart.

"I have a previous engagement. I won't be home till quite late." Sean hadn't said yes or no, just that he wasn't available. Sean wanted out of this conversation.

"I'm sorry. May I see you tomorrow? I will see you tomorrow… for breakfast. You promised me breakfast." Coleman was scrambling. He could feel Sean slipping away.

"You said you'd be here for breakfast this morning." Sean wasn't sure why he'd said that.

"I'm sorry, I should have called. I'm sorry. When are you leaving? I want to see you. We need to talk." Coleman was demanding now.

"I'm leaving now. It's okay, I know already, you don't have to tell me. I have to go. Good-bye." He did not want to talk, and he didn't want to hear what Coleman was going to tell him. Sean was emotionally spent by the time he hung up the phone. It was tiring trying to pretend he was unaffected by him. In a few months, maybe a year, he would be able to forget Coleman. He needed to talk to Ed; he needed to get this sorted out as fast as possible.

Coleman felt crushed. All the joy and satisfaction he'd felt over the completion of the merger was gone; all that remained was painful regret and a helpless panic. He tried to figure out what Sean had meant by "I know already, you don't have to tell me." What did he know already? Relationships were completely new to him, and he wasn't experienced in how to care for a lover. But he would have to learn fast, and the first step would be not to wait a week to call someone after they spent the weekend with you. He was so used to relationships being strictly sexual and completely on his terms he still wasn't certain what he wanted from Sean in the long run, but he knew for sure he didn't want it to end.

The gallery exhibition was wonderful, and so were the art and the artists. Sean enjoyed just walking among it all, and it was nice having Mr. Murray with him.

They stopped to admire an intricate sculpture of a sea creature, and Ed decided it was time to ask. "So, Sean, why is it you invited me and not Coleman? What's going on? I'm not complaining, you are a wonderful companion, but your interest definitely lies elsewhere, and we both know it." Ed gave him that look that said, "Time to spill."

Sean swallowed hard before speaking and didn't maintain eye contact although Ed was watching him very closely. "It's over—he's finished with me."

"Did he tell you that?"

"Didn't have to. He hasn't spoken to me since last weekend. He was supposed to have breakfast with me this morning, but he didn't show up. I didn't think he would, considering." The more he talked, the more he realized he still had very deep, hurt feelings with regard to Coleman. It dawned on him then that perhaps he would never get over him. Coleman would be the relationship that was always there, always remembered, always relived.

"Considering what?" Ed was focused and wanted the whole story. He didn't trust Coleman, but he found it unlikely he would abandon Sean so soon. But then, what did he know? Coleman had a terrible and hurtful reputation, and it didn't surprise Ed that he would simply drop someone without a thought or a care for their feelings in the matter.

"I saw him Friday night. I was out for a walk, and I saw him get out of one of his cars and there was this guy with him. They went into a restaurant together; Coleman had his hand on his shoulder, and he looked really happy, pleased. The guy was gorgeous, definitely cream of the crop." Sean closed his eyes, willing the tears away. "He had time to take this guy to dinner, but he didn't have time to call me."

"I'm sorry, kid." Ed put his arm around Sean's shoulders and squeezed him sympathetically. "Life can be a bitch."

"Thanks, Mr. Murray."

"You know, Sean, considering we are on a date, and I would hazard to guess that more than half the people in this room believe us to be a couple, it would be okay for you to call me Ed.' They both broke out laughing hysterically.

Coleman arrived at his apartment at nine and found that he was constantly slamming things, the door, the closet, the cupboard, until finally, he took a vase from the hall end table and threw it so hard against the living room wall that it smashed into pieces. It eased his exasperation a little, but he could not stop thinking about Sean and wondering what he was doing and who he was with. He wanted to call Sean again, but he knew he needed to leave him alone, for the night, anyway. He would call in the morning and see him at his apartment or at work. One way or another, he was going to talk to him; they would work this out. He vowed he would never again take Sean for granted. Had he kept in touch, had he remembered to take Sean's feelings into consideration, had he thought about someone other than himself and his work, this would not be happening. All week he had been so sure, so confident in everything he was doing. In his mind he believed Sean was his. He was in love with Sean and it filled him with peace, but in reality, he'd never said any of that to Sean. The only thing Sean knew was that Coleman hadn't spoken to him in a week, and he'd stood Sean up for their breakfast date. He stomped around the place for another two hours before going to bed.

Ed and Sean left the exhibition around ten. On the ride back to drop Sean off at his apartment, Ed asked him how he felt about going to work in the morning.

"I wish I could hide for a few days."

"I have a case that needs a deposition completed in Detroit—you're welcome to go. It will take about two days to complete, and by then, perhaps things will be better." Ed was aware of the level of discomfort Sean was experiencing and wanted to give him an opportunity to escape, at least for a few days.

Sean's eyes brightened. "Thank you, Ed. When can I leave?" He jumped on the offer so quickly Ed started to laugh.

"A car will pick you up at ten in the morning."

"You are the greatest."

"Of course I am." Ed smiled. He was glad he was able to give the kid a little relief, although he would still have to deal with the heartache when he returned. But his internship would be over in another two weeks, and then he would be able to put Coleman behind him and go on with his life.

The call came as soon as he got home. Weir was upset and he wasn't hiding it. "Sean, I am very disappointed in you. How could you think that this kind of behavior was in any way acceptable?" He was almost yelling.

"What are you talking about?" Sean hoped Weir didn't know the extent of his relationship with Coleman. The evening with Ed had been so relaxing, as was the idea of going out of town for a few days. Dealing with Weir as soon as Sean got home was just too much.

"I received a call saying that you have been engaging in inappropriate behavior with... with a superior at the Firm." Weir was definitely yelling now.

"Who called?" Sean was not as angry or upset as he should have been. It was inevitable, and he found that he actually felt resigned to the fact that his placement was about to be terminated. That was the risk he had taken when he got involved with Coleman. When Coleman was through with someone, he was completely through. Coleman had called Weir, Sean knew that much. He called him so he could get rid of Sean without having to do it himself. Sean's insolent behavior with him when he called earlier probably put a rush on his dismissal.

"It doesn't matter who called, what matters is that you are making a mockery of every intern who has ever been placed at the firm. I don't think I have to tell you that your placement is finished." Professor Weir sounded very pleased.

"Yes, sir."

"I want you back in Mt. Pleasant by tomorrow, and we will discuss your future in this program."

"Yes, sir."

Sean made himself a cup of tea and sat down in the living room to contemplate all the actions that had led to his present situation. He did not go to bed that night. Instead, he cleaned. The apartment looked as if no one had ever lived in it by the time Sean was finished. He took his backpack and messenger bag and placed them by the front door. He had already called the bus station and bought his ticket back to Mt. Pleasant. The bus was leaving at 6:30 a.m., and the station was about a half-hour walk from his apartment, so he would have to leave by five thirty at the latest.

He'd called Ed right after he ended his call with Weir and told him what had happened. Ed offered to call Weir and try and reason with him, but Sean had asked him not to. "It is pretty obvious who called, so anything you try to do to help me would only be held against you in the end. It is not worth it, Ed," Sean told him. Ed wanted to do something, but he would not go against Sean's wishes. He offered to give him a ride to the station, but Sean wanted to walk, wanted to have the time to calm and to clear himself. Ed asked Sean for his address in Mt. Pleasant because he wanted to come and see him later in the week. Then he wished him luck and told him not to let it get to him. "Take from it what you can use and discard the rest," he advised.

"I will, and thank you, sir." Sean had gotten choked up, so he'd said good-bye and got busy cleaning the apartment.

Now he stood at the door and looked into the apartment. It was a nice place, and he appreciated that Coleman had provided this for him. He would also cherish the moments that had felt so real, and the acceptance. Those memories would get him through the next few weeks, anyway, he told himself as he closed the door and left.

Coleman was up before dawn and out of his apartment by seven. He was determined to meet with Sean before work. He'd tossed and turned all night, trying to figure out what he should say and do in order for Sean to understand how much he meant to him. Once Sean finished his internship, Coleman would enroll Sean at the art academy, and he would move him into his apartment and the country home. He would have Sean move his things from Mt.

Pleasant, and hopefully, he could convince him to sell the home he had lived in with his mother and inherited from her and relocate to Chicago permanently. Coleman considered calling him first and then decided to just show up. He wanted to see Sean; he needed to talk to him.

Coleman stood outside Sean's apartment and knocked and rang the bell until finally he walked away, unsure whether he was being ignored or if Sean had already left for work. The knot in his stomach tightened, and he ran his hand through his hair, agitated with himself and his inability to deal with this. He walked swiftly into the building and headed straight for the third floor and Ed Murray's office. He needed to sort this out.

"Good morning, Ed, is Sean in back?" Coleman moved quickly past Ed on his way to the back office that Sean used for research.

"He's not here." Ed stood up, surprised to see Coleman here so early

Coleman stopped immediately and turned to regard Ed with a glare "Where is he?"

"On his way home, I believe," Ed said carefully as Coleman walked toward him, studying his every word. "Weir terminated his placement last night. Someone called and said he was engaging in inappropriate behavior."

Coleman stood silent, the anger he felt radiating off his body. "Why didn't he call me?" he gritted out between clenched teeth.

Ed scrutinized Coleman closely, trying to discern the truth of what he was saying. Coleman didn't appear to be a man who didn't care. "He believes it was you who reported him."

Coleman lost his composure for a moment as shock ran through him. "Why the hell would he believe that?" he hissed.

"He has heard all of the rumors and stories about you, and on top of that, you ignored him for a week, you stood him up, and he saw you with that man Friday night. As far as he knows, it's over, you're through with him." Ed watched as Coleman struggled to comprehend everything he'd just said. "He called me last night and told me his placement had been terminated, and he had to be back in Mt. Pleasant today to meet with Weir. He understood being dumped by you, he could eventually deal with that, but he couldn't comprehend the meanness of you having him kicked out of the program."

"I didn't dump him, and I didn't report him. I would never hurt him, Ed. I called him yesterday on my way back from Minneapolis. I wanted to see him, but he told me he had a previous commitment. I should have called him sooner; I just assumed he would be here waiting for me." Coleman felt the need to try and explain himself to Ed.

"He was with me. We went to the Morgan for the art exhibition. I think he just needed to get out and talk to someone."

"He could have talked to me."

"He didn't see it that way." Ed felt compassion begin to rise in him for the man standing before him, obviously shocked by what he was hearing. "I offered to intercede, but he said, 'We both know who called Weir, so please don't do anything because it will just make life harder for you.'" Seeing the pain flash across Coleman's face, Ed reached out and placed his hand on Coleman's arm in a comforting gesture he would never even have considered in the past, but right now the man looked devastated.

"Friday night I was at the Regency for dinner with James Tobin, the lead attorney for Buckland. It was all business. The man is married and has two children. I was not on a date. What did he see?" Coleman stiffened a little and tried to remember anything Sean could have seen that would have led him to believe it was a date.

"He told me, 'He had time to take this guy to dinner, but he didn't have time to call me. Yes, he is definitely finished with me.' He thinks you called and made the report to Weir because you just didn't want to have to look at him anymore."

Coleman stepped back and dragged his hand through his hair, distressed and disconcerted, and not sure what his next step should be. "I'm not finished, Ed, not by a long shot." He straightened, and the cold, calculating Coleman West was back. His presence changed in an instant from confused to focused.

"He gave me his address in Mt. Pleasant. Would you like to have it?" Ed asked before handing him the note.

"Thanks, Ed." Coleman took the note and put it in his pocket. "I love Sean, I adore him, but I haven't cared about anyone but myself my entire life, so I'm having difficulty doing this right. I need him, Ed. I can't lose him, not over a misunderstanding, not over anything... I won't accept it." He'd shared more personal information about himself with Ed in these few minutes together than he'd ever shared with anyone. Ed was Sean's closest friend here in Chicago, so he needed Ed to know his true intentions. He needed Ed on his side if he had any hope of getting Sean to trust him.

"He's in a bad place right now, feeling abandoned by you and victimized by Weir. If you truly want to fix this, you will have to do something quickly. Don't wait," Ed advised as gently but firmly as he felt he was allowed to.

"I want to fix this, and I assure you I will not be waiting." Coleman left the office and stormed up to the eighth floor. Everyone who met him in the hall quickly got out of his way. It got around fast that the boss was back and he was furious. The latest gossip was that it had something to do with the intern, Sean Robbins, but no one was sure what had happened. Jason was the only person brave enough to approach him.

"What's going on, Coleman, that you have the entire floor in panic mode?"

"Sean's gone."

"Gone?"

"Someone here called Weir and reported him for inappropriate behavior, and his placement was terminated."

Jason stood silent for a few moments. "Who would be brash enough to do such a thing?"

"I don't know, but I will find out." Coleman walked over to his desk, grabbed the phone, and dialed the university in Mt. Pleasant. He spoke with the president of the board of regents and threatened to remove his support for the university should Weir not be dealt with. He then moved directly to Weir. Jason remained in the room, listening as Coleman very coldly and determinedly took the professor apart.

"You will call him immediately and explain your mistake, and then you will tell him he has completed his placement. You will give him full credit for the three months and will sign and present him with his certificate. You will do this today before five. If you do not, I will see to it that you never work at another school in this country or any other. Do I make myself clear?" He hung up the phone and walked over to where Jason was standing.

"I assume that's been cleared up," Jason stated with suppressed humor.

"He wouldn't have had the balls to even try this if Sean had let me slap him down the first time he gave him grief. Always remember: when you give an inch, you risk losing a mile. Sean is too nice for his own good, always extending second chances to people who don't deserve them." His expression became thoughtful as he continued, "I can only hope he will extend me the same courtesy."

"Who called him?" Jason interjected into his thoughts

"No one. He made it up in order to control Sean. He knew something was going on, he just couldn't prove it, so he invented a snitch."

"What's going on?" Jason knew he was treading on dangerous ground, but he wanted to know if this is just another short-termer or if Coleman really had feelings for Sean. Sean didn't deserve to be brought back here just to be dumped again in a week or two. He decided to blurt it out. "You know, if you can't offer Sean something substantial, you really have no right to bring him back here."

Coleman did not immediately respond. Jason's concern for Sean surprised him. "I don't know where this is going to ultimately lead, but I do know that I can't lose him. I've never in my life had feelings like the feelings I have for Sean. I don't want to even imagine my life without him. I don't know what he feels for me, if anything, but I need to tell him how I feel, what I need, and what he means to me." Coleman did not elaborate beyond that declaration, but it was enough to convince Jason.

"Well, then, good luck and go bring him back," Jason stated with a smile. "I'll take care of everything here so take your time."

"Thanks." Coleman stormed out of his office and called his pilot on his way out the door.

TWELVE

SEAN arrived at the bus stop in downtown Mt. Pleasant at eleven, and he still had to walk quite a distance home. He could have called Tom, a friend of his from the club to pick him up, but he didn't feel in the mood to answer all of the questions they would most certainly have. The nearly one-mile walk to his home on the edge of town took him roughly twenty minutes. He was glad to see his home and have a chance to disappear inside it, for a while, anyway. Although his mother was no longer there to help him through a difficult time like this, his home was always a comfort to him. He put the key in the lock and opened the door. Inside it was calm and friendly and welcoming. Sean tossed his backpack and messenger bag on the sofa and went to the kitchen for a glass of water before taking a tour of the house to make sure everything was in good order. He'd had Tom checking on the place while he was gone. He would have to call him and let him know he was home. Hopefully, he wouldn't question Sean about it. Then Sean went back to the living room and sat down on the end of the sofa, away from his bags, and placed the glass of water on the coffee table positioned in front of the sofa. Leaning back and rubbing his face with his hands, he considered his options.

With regard Weir, Sean knew he would not grovel, and he would not be placed in a subservient position. *He can do whatever he wants*, Sean decided, *I will not beg and will not be made to do anything not in my own best interests.* He would have to call Weir soon and arrange for a meeting. He wasn't looking forward to dealing with the man; he had a tendency as of late to be rather crass, and it wasn't a good look on him. His behavior was causing him to appear as less of a man in Sean's eyes. Sean thought about the things Coleman had said about Weir, and suddenly, he was willing to believe the accusations were probably true. Weir's recent conduct was indicative of a man out for his own satisfaction. When Weir spoke to Sean on the phone, he hadn't even asked if the accusations were true; he'd just taken it as an opportunity to make him squirm. Although if he had asked, Sean realized he would not have lied. He would have confessed that, yes indeed, he was having an affair with Coleman West. Sean might have even shared with Weir what an amazing lover Coleman was, so attentive and considerate of his partner. The statement made him smile and then made him sad. Coleman was someone he would never forget and would probably never get over.

Enough of that, he told himself, time to get back to his options. He needed to stop mooning over Coleman. He had treated Sean like gold until he was finished with him and then had treated him like shit. Coleman, like Weir, was not worth Sean's time or energy.

He still had his art degree and part of a legal-assistant certificate. What would that combination get him, he wondered. He could get a job at the bar again, and maybe even work more hours. They served food, so he could possibly work in the kitchen and work cleanup. That would see him through until something better came along. Sean decided to call Mr. Anderson at the bar and secure a job before calling Weir and setting up the meeting. He would be in a stronger place if he walked in knowing he had a job to fall back on.

His mind wandered back to Coleman and the time they had spent together. It had only been a few weeks, but it changed him, probably forever. Would Coleman think about him? Or had he already forgotten all about him and moved on with his social life. *He's probably planning his time with the new guy and has completely forgotten about me. Yes, he has forgotten... that's who he is*, Sean chastised himself. *He doesn't do relationships. He stays as long as it is entertaining and fresh, and then he leaves. He does not tolerate clinging vines, and he will destroy anyone who doesn't know enough to let go when it is over.* Ed had told him that much, as well as Jason, and now Sean knew it to be true. *He didn't even give me a chance to walk away. He just tossed me and my career aside without a thought or a care, as usual. He told me he would never deliberately hurt me, but that turned out to be a lie, like everything else he told me. Oh well, better a clean break than wandering around waiting for the end to come in small doses; no, better a punch to the gut than slow, drawn-out torture.* "Enough," Sean said out loud and then made his call to the bar

Coleman landed at the airport in Mt. Pleasant at eleven thirty and rented a car at the counter. He took the address Ed had given him and programmed it into the mapping system in the car. He needed to get to Sean as soon as possible. It tore his heart to think Sean believed he had been discarded, cast off, abandoned by Coleman. He couldn't imagine living his life without Sean in it. That thought brought a realization of what he truly wanted from Sean. He'd been telling everyone he wasn't sure what he wanted out of this relationship, but that was not the truth. He knew exactly what he wanted from Sean. He wanted his love, his time, his presence, his future. He belonged to Sean, and Sean belonged to him. He'd never even considered that Sean would not be there waiting for him when he returned from Minneapolis. In his mind, their relationship was solid; in his mind there was already a commitment.

It had all happened that night in Cleveland. Bonds had been forged and futures were set. Coleman saw Sean clearly that night, and he'd been overwhelmed by what he saw. Sean had become everything that night. Until then, he had believed what he felt for Sean was special, but not permanent. Coleman had believed the time would come when he would want to move on and find someone new, but that night he'd realized he would never let Sean go; he would never release him. Coleman wanted to kick himself for not making that clear to Sean. For all Sean knew, their relationship had been temporary. Sean had heard all the rumors and knew who he was, and based on all of that distorted information, he would naturally conclude Coleman was finished with him. Coleman sighed.

"I'M VERY sorry, Sean. Apparently I got the whole thing wrong." Weir was apologetic and Sean was having difficulty understanding what was going on. Weir was calling very late and sounded almost frightened.

"What do you mean?"

"I must have misunderstood the caller. I am sorry and I will make restitution to you." Weir sounded almost afraid. His voice was rapid and broken.

"Restitution?"

"Yes, I thought perhaps I would go ahead and issue you your certificate of completion." Weir paused, then added, "Coleman West has already agreed to sign it as is. You will have completed the course."

"I don't have to finish the internship?"

"You have finished the program. And I will issue you your certificate. When can you be at my office to pick it up? I'd like to be home before five tomorrow." Then he added, "No, wait, I'll drop it off." Weir then hung up it was as if he couldn't wait to get off the phone.

Coleman must have had a burst of conscience to agree to sign off on his certification. Sean wanted to tell him to stick it up his ass, but he wouldn't be speaking to Coleman anytime soon, or anytime at all, for that matter. Sean decided to accept it and move on. With his certificate, he could hopefully apply somewhere around Mt. Pleasant for a job. He owned his own home, and financially, that would be the best option for him right now.

Sean picked up his glass of water and grabbed his laptop from his bag, then moved over to the desk near the television. He was scanning the "Help Wanted" ads when his doorbell began to ring and then was followed by an insistent knocking. Whoever it was, they were definitely impatient.

"Just a minute," Sean barked as he stood up and approached his front door. He was wondering who it could be, and then remembered Weir was coming over to give him his certificate. "Damn," he mumbled under his breath. He really didn't feel in the mood to talk with that man. Maybe Weir would slip it through the mail slot and leave. But no, good manners dictated that Sean open the door and speak with him. He used to have such respect and admiration for Weir, but ever since the setup at the luncheon for intern placement, followed by the creepy phone call in Cleveland, he had developed a very different opinion of the professor. Sean planned to take his certificate and then close the door. No need for pleasantries at this stage of the game.

Sean swung open the door with aggressive intent but was struck numb with shock and disbelief when he came face to face with Coleman. His brain tried to understand and come to terms with Coleman standing on his front porch in Mt. Pleasant. It didn't make sense, so he blinked several times, hoping to clear his vision. Then he backed up slightly, not sure how to handle this.

"Sean." Coleman stepped toward him but then stopped. "I'm sorry." He looked as though he wanted to say so much more, but "I'm sorry" was all his mind could muster at the moment.

"Why are you here?" Sean bit out with barely suppressed anger. He drew his lips into a tight line and stared at Coleman, challenging him. Sean decided instantly that he was not going to take any shit from this guy. Sean was through treating Coleman like he mattered. Coleman did not matter anymore. He could say and do whatever he wanted; Sean refused to be affected. Maybe Coleman would decline to sign off his internship, but right now Sean didn't care. He was done with games and living his life by other peoples' rules.

"May I come in?" Coleman said softly and took another tentative step toward the door.

"No." Sean surprised himself with that statement. "I don't have time for small talk. I'm busy."

"Please, Sean, don't shut me out. I'm begging you. Please talk to me." Coleman implored him to listen to him. His eyes pleaded as he reached out to him. "Please, Sean, let me in."

Sean stepped back from the door and motioned him inside. He found he was too overcome with emotion to speak just then. Hearing Coleman's soft, emotional plea both confused and touched him. He hoped he wouldn't regret letting Coleman in. Sean did not look at him as he walked into the living room and Coleman followed him.

Sean turned to him but kept his gaze on the floor. "What do you want?" he finally said, but his voice was tense with emotion.

Coleman moved toward him with his hand still outstretched, but Sean reacted by stepping back. He wasn't ready to be touched.

"I didn't call Weir. I didn't abandon you. I should have called you sooner. I want you back." Every emotion that entered Coleman's mind came out of his mouth in awkward, blunt statements and demands. He pushed his hands through his hair, frustrated and angry at his own inability to make himself clear. Standing there staring at Sean, Coleman panicked at the way Sean disregarded him. Sean wouldn't look at him—since he first opened the door he had refused to look at him. "Damn it Sean! Look at me!"

"What am I supposed to see?" Sean asked coolly.

"The person who is in love with you," Coleman stated plainly.

These were not words Sean had expected to hear. Sean always kept him at arm's length, as getting close was too dangerous. But hearing those words flipped something in him. Coleman was serious. This was no game.

"You mean that?"

"I would never lie to you," Coleman stated before moving forward and taking Sean in his arms.

The arms felt like home, a place Sean had been missing for a long time. He nuzzled in, loving the scent and strength of Coleman.

"I'll never let you go again," Coleman said as he smiled in relief.

"That's something I could live with," Sean said, leaning in for a kiss.

EPILOGUE

SEAN sat at the counter in the kitchen of Coleman's country estate... *their* country estate, he corrected himself. Coleman had been pressing him for weeks now to call the home theirs. It had been almost a year since that moment in his living room in Mt. Pleasant. The moment he finally believed Coleman, finally knew Coleman wasn't playing with him. How could he deny it when he heard the three words Coleman had never said to anyone? Sean smiled and sipped his coffee. Life had gotten pretty damn good. He still had small moments of doubt, but all he had to do was see the adoration in Coleman's face and all doubt and fear disappeared. Coleman stepped up behind him and enveloped Sean in his arms.

"What are you thinking about so seriously?" Coleman asked as he placed a tender kiss on Sean's cheek.

"I never thought things could be this good. Things like this never happen to me," Sean said thoughtfully.

"Well, believe it. I never plan on saying good-bye to you." Coleman squeezed him tighter and then released him as he dug into the pocket of his overcoat that hung near the back door.

Sean was puzzled. "What's that?"

Coleman walked to him and took Sean's hands in his own. "I wanted to do this in a crazy, grand, romantic way, but that isn't us. This is us—a simple, quiet morning; a simple, quiet, loving existence." Coleman paused and looked to be gathering his nerve. Sean was confused; Coleman never had to steady his nerves.

"I can't tell you how happy you've made me. I never want this to end; I never want to lose you." Coleman paused again. "To that end... I want you to make me the happiest man in the world and marry me."

Sean's jaw dropped and his breath caught in his throat. His eyes welled up with tears and he couldn't believe what he was hearing. Coleman West—the take no prisoners, didn't believe in love head of Coleman West and Associates Law Firm—was asking him to marry him. He could only give one answer.

"Yes. A thousand times yes." Sean was crying now as Coleman placed the ring on his finger and pulled him into a firm, loving embrace.

"You're never allowed to leave me," Coleman said as he kissed Sean.

"That's a deal I can agree to." Sean smiled widely.

His and Coleman's lips met once more. He planned on staying like that forever.

B.A. STRETKE began writing when a fifth grade teacher told him he couldn't. That same stubbornness and drive led to the discovery of an actual talent. B.A. spends his days reading, engaging in sarcasm, and plotting ways to trap a rich Canadian husband so he can buy his mother a Lamborghini. He has dreams of being a schoolteacher and a novelist, as well as having a closet big enough to hold his obsessive collection of cardigans. B.A. writes to escape the mundane small town life—that same drive to write the great American novel never dying.

B.A. Stretke lives in Sault Ste. Marie, Michigan, with two royally spoiled cats and his dear friends and family.

B.A. tweets at twitter.com/DramaticPause10 and blogs at www.mypridemarch.net.

Also from B.A. STRETKE

http://www.dreamspinnerpress.com

Also in Italian and Spanish

http://www.dreamspinnerpress.com

Romance from DREAMSPINNER PRESS

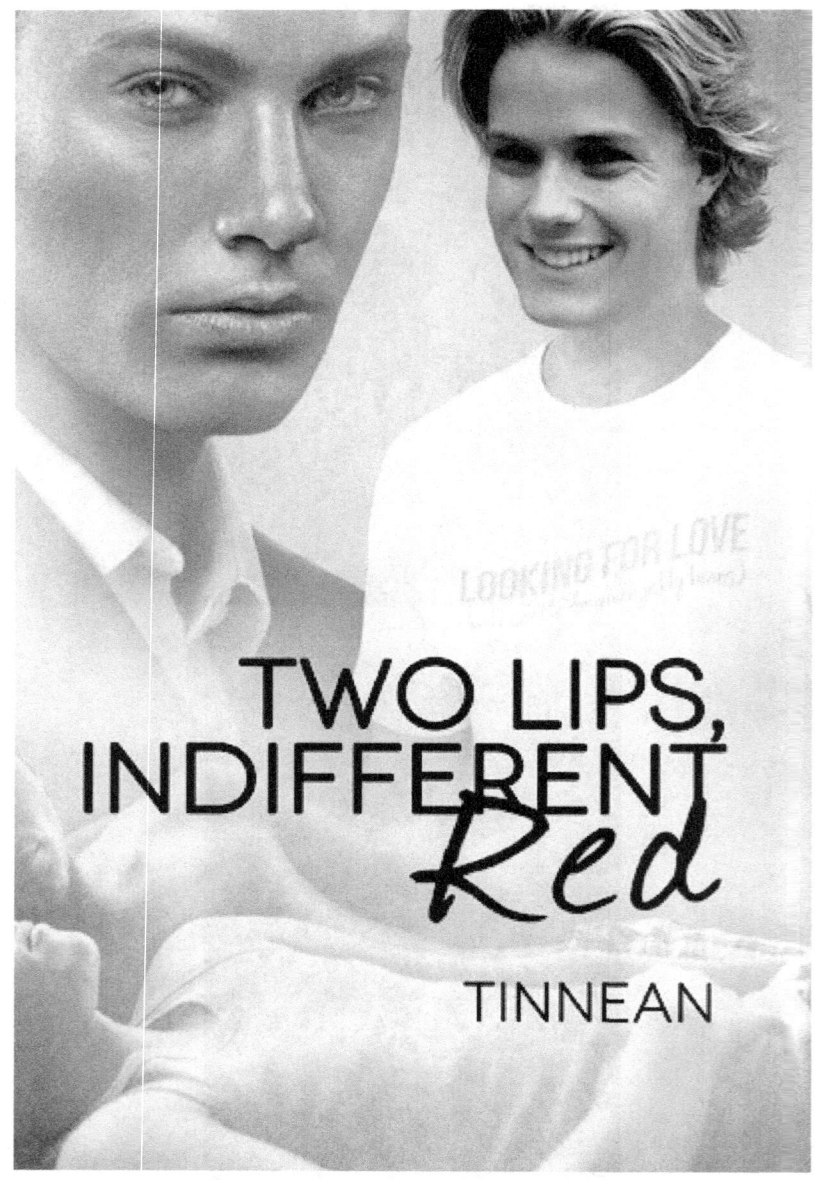

LOOKING FOR LOVE

TWO LIPS, INDIFFERENT *Red*

TINNEAN

http://www.dreamspinnerpress.com

http://www.dreamspinnerpress.com

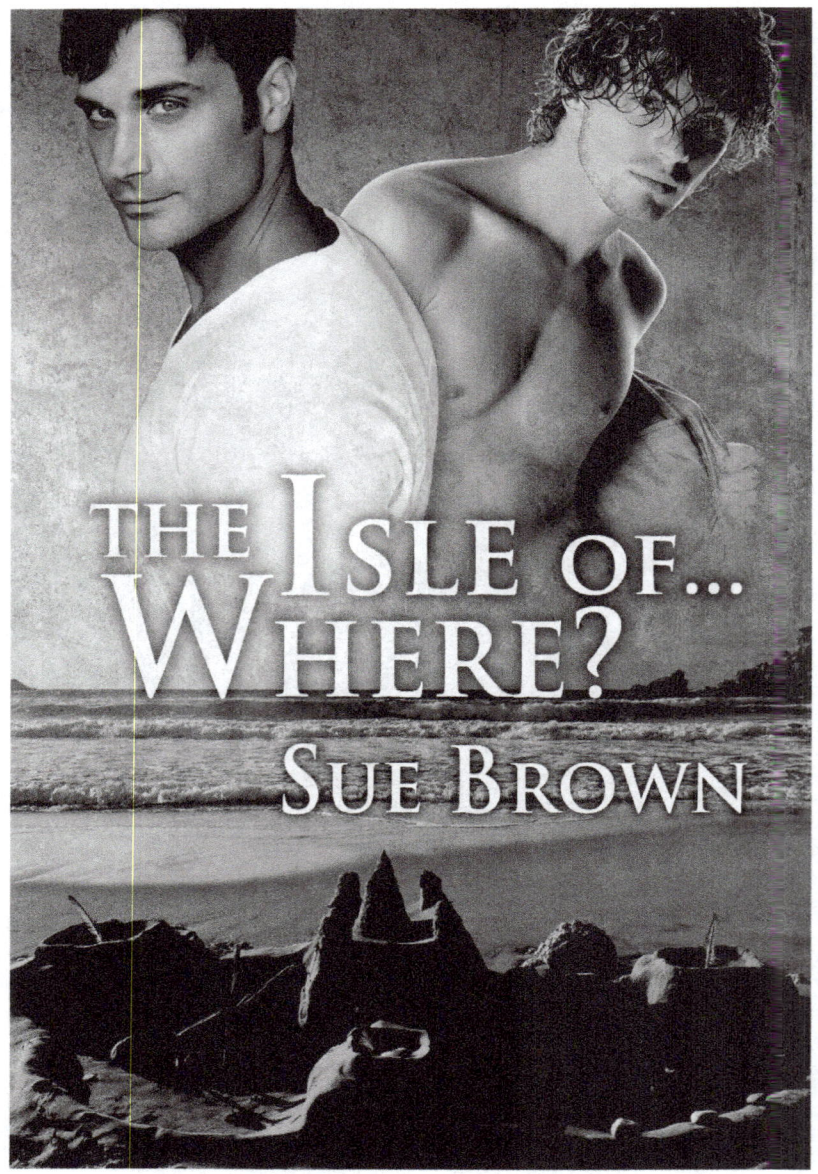

THE ISLE OF...
WHERE?

SUE BROWN

Romance from DREAMSPINNER PRESS

HOSTILE TAKEOVER

EM LYNLEY

http://www.dreamspinnerpress.com

Made in United States
Orlando, FL
22 March 2026

79557641R00115